M000034482

ca re

stories

care

stories

CHRISTOPHER RECORDS

Inlandia Books

Care: Stories
Copyright © 2020 by Christopher Records
ISBN: 978-1-7324032-7-7
Library of Congress Control Number: 2020933801
All rights reserved

No part of this book may be used, reproduced, or adapted to public
performances in any manner whatsoever without permission from
both the publisher and the copyright owner, except in the case of
brief quotations embodied in critical articles and reviews. For more
information, write to Permissions, Inlandia Institute, 4178 Chestnut Street
Riverside CA 92501.

Cover art: Sergii Radkevych
Book design and layout: Kenji C. Liu

Printed and bound in the United States
Distributed by Ingram

Published by Inlandia Institute
Riverside, California
www.InlandiaInstitute.org
First Edition

Less the rescue.
More, always, the ache
toward it.

— Carl Phillips

CONTENTS

AUTHOR'S NOTE

I wrote this collection at a time when I was reckoning with the end of certain long-held assumptions I'd held about my life, values, society, and this country. The distress and anxiety that I felt in the spring and summer of 2017 are evident in the twelve stories that comprise this book.

The image of the future that they present is a country defined by isolation and stagnation, millions of people rendered socially and economically useless, political and cultural corruption seeping into ordinary lives and relationships and degrading them, and a turn toward easy and destructive solutions to complicated, messy problems. Two years later, that picture has only grown more vivid and more resonant to me.

I wanted to see these forces at work in the lives of people I could recognize. I wanted to tell the stories of ordinary queer people living ordinary lives in an ordinary place.

The Inland Empire of Southern California is where I grew up, was educated, came out, first fell in love. It's a place that I think gets a bad rap, especially considering that it's one of the only parts of Southern California where a genuine middle class still exists. The stories in *Care* are set in the Inland Empire not because I wanted to portray the region in a negative light, but because I wanted to explore what my community might look like ten or twenty years in the future.

At the center of all these stories lies the desire for escape and the longing for catharsis that we all feel living in a world in which neat, tidy endings are often elusive. America exists because of these things. I expect that it will die of the same causes.

I am grateful to Cati Porter of Inlandia for her advocacy of this book and her patience with the process of editing it; to my editor, Robert Merrill, for his incisive feedback; and to Ryan Lo for everything else.

FROM YOU

Ontario

She is back, the tall woman. The tall woman always comes in wanting something, always comes in concerned. She always wants something from me, some assurance. She's always concerned because I never give it to her. I have nothing more to give.

Today is no different. She's come in the evening, after work or something. I assume it's work or something else that matters. Something where people are waiting on her. Something where her response is required, where her words have authority.

She comes in when it's quiet outside except for the ambient hum of the freeway and the sun going down. She says nothing and looks at me, and I say nothing and look away. She sits down and waits for something to happen.

My eyes throb behind my closed eyelids as we breathe loudly in our separate places. The sun is too bright and coming in through the blinds in a way that emphasizes decay, that draws attention to the dust in the air and the stains on the walls and the wrinkles on our faces. I feel it without looking at it. I feel the weight of her worry, her dogged hope that I'll tell her something she wants to hear. Minutes pass. Nothing.

"You've got to eat, Sandra," she says. It's the same thing she says every time.

"No, I don't, June," I say, my eyes open. "Think I've proven that by now."

And I have. It's been three weeks since I've eaten, since I touched the meals that they've been diligently preparing for me since I came here nine months ago. I'm proud of it, even though there's nothing, really, to be proud of. It's easy. I've had a lifetime of practice starving myself. It's not been that hard to take it one step further.

I mean, what is it? Forgoing. Not doing. Easy. I'm good at not doing. What do I not do? An activity I've never taken much pleasure in anyway. No matter what I've eaten in the past sixty-something years, I've never eaten it without a thought or two about how much better I would look and feel without having eaten it.

Hunger has been as constant in my life as doubt and shame and fear. It is not difficult for me to give in to it now at the end. To embrace it, to chain myself to it. It is a manageable emotion. It is more comfortable than so many others.

The tall woman braces herself on the arms of the metal chair. I look at her in the half-light, at the carefully made up, symmetrical face with its sharp cheekbones and the gray curls, close-cut to the scalp. I look at the body beneath the face, which I should know like my own for however many times I've seen and felt and smelled and tasted it, but which looks, from this vantage point, like the body of any strange, old woman on the street. I look, through the pain that shoots through my stomach and the small of my back and my breasts and the part of my arm where they've inserted the IV that keeps me tethered to this place. I look and I hurt. It's all I do these days.

"You look terrible," she says.

"I feel worse."

It's honestly quite good to hurt now, to feel my body as something sharp and poisonous, to be pulled down into it, into my throbbing kidneys and my sore bowels and my aching back and my raw throat and mouth. It's good to feel my private parts burning in the morning, to gather my arms across my chest and press and wince because my heart is frenzied and struggling. Hurting, I become stupid. Hurting, I become calm. I prefer to feel these things than to feel what came before. I prefer to know that they will produce a

2

result that I want rather than just another day, week, month, year of this.

"Why are you doing this?" she asks me.

"To get away," I reply.

"From what?"

"From you," I smile. It's the same thing I told her when I checked into this place.

PRAISEWORTHY

Palm Springs

That last night before they went off to the center, after they'd finished signing the title transfer to their car and accepted the $1400 that the man from Craigslist was willing to pay for it, Ilan suddenly realized that it would be the last night that they would enjoy the freedom to choose what and whom the night would be about and made a snap decision to have sex with someone. They opened the app and tried to find a man. It usually took work, hours of it, time cajoling and convincing, giving up and then having another go at it. It usually resulted in someone who was less than ideal, someone flawed. This time, blessedly, miraculously, it took 15 minutes and yielded a man who was more than acceptable for the purpose Ilan had in mind, one who lived less than a mile away.

Ilan didn't know what to wear. It had just rained. Heavily. It was winter rain in the desert, hot and cold all at once, unreliable, uneven, catching people unprepared, mingling with sweat, coaxing more of it out of the skin. It was hard to dress for it. They didn't have an umbrella, hadn't thought to keep one around. There wasn't one in their empty apartment.

It was too wet for sandals. It was too hot for boots. They had their choice of one or the other with everything else in boxes that were en route to Vegas. They put on boots and socks and long pants and a sweatshirt. They looked like they would look going to any date or evening assignation in any other city. Dressed to impress for long enough, and then to easily unclothe themselves. They started dripping into the clothes before they left the apartment.

They had hoped to hail a cab to avoid becoming even more uncomfortable, but none passed. Just an endless stream of people here for the festival, rich, young people from Shanghai and Buenos Aires and LA and Cape Town and New York and London and St. Petersburg. It was six in the evening.

The app man told them that he could either meet now, in the two hours between the end of work and dinner plans that the man had with family, or much later in the evening, probably around midnight.

Ilan had decided not to pretend not to be eager; they told him that they'd be over in ten minutes. They weren't comfortable with moving around the city, any city, late at night. After midnight, things could happen. After midnight, already vulnerable people became even more vulnerable. And they didn't want to wait. They were nervous at the possibility of a cancellation, at the loss of this one last opportunity. More time meant more possibilities, more options. They didn't like changed plans. They didn't like the idea of spending another four or five hours on the app, trying to track down someone acceptable and willing, or of feeling even more unattractively desperate when they failed. There was a particular kind of desperation that came with trolling for sex at two or three a.m. It caused knots in the stomach and lightness in the head. It caused them to feel like they were far from themselves, like they were in danger of falling off the edge of something, the edge of normal behavior, the edge of sanity.

So now it was. Now.

They started jogging down the street, snaking through groups of people huddled under the awnings, sitting at streetside cafes with cigarettes and glasses of booze. A woman in a loose sundress with her hands tucked pensively behind her back appeared in front of them; they ran past her. The edge of her dress fluttered from the breeze their body caused. They sped around cars stopped at a light, shaving off the minute or two that might have been spent at a crosswalk. They made the mile from the apartment to the man's place in six minutes as the sun settled somewhere under the mountains.

Ilan's eyes scanned the identical '70s squat brown apartments on Tahquitz Canyon, their destination. Google

Maps tracked their movements, and they tried to match the buildings on the screen to the buildings in front of them. The rain started up again, and they began running, kicking up the water on the street, dirtying their shoes and pants, their forehead and back dripping. They rounded a corner and nearly crashed into a blonde couple walking arm and arm in the opposite direction. The anger in the man's German scratched the back of their ears as they ran away.

Ilan found the correct building anointed with graffiti, its side marked with a gigantic red "ANTIFA." The three women and their babies eyed Ilan suspiciously as they edged around a small wall made of strollers and bodies. Ilan reread the instructions on the phone, buzzed the name that they'd been given, checking and then double-checking the letters to ensure they'd identified the correct one. A Greek nude greeted them in the lobby. It was an archaic kouros with a passive smile and large, vacant eyes and dreadlocks and square kneecaps. They jogged up the steep steps while typing "I'm here" on the phone screen.

There was a long pause in the dark on the fourth floor, where the man had told them the apartment was located. As usual, they considered the possibility that it was a fake-out, a joke, an extortion attempt, that a group of young men were waiting on the other end of one of the doors to rush out and pile on and beat and rob them or worse.

But then a door opened, and the man appeared.

He was pantsless but had a shirt on. Collared, open, revealing lots of chest hair. There was a tattoo on his right breast. Red, Chinese characters. Ilan could make out a few shapes at the front end and none of the rest; the hair was too dark there. His legs were long and sinewy and tan and covered in dark hairs, and his feet were bare; there was another tattoo on the left one, a quarter-sized red rose.

He looked the age that he had advertised—36. He looked much better in person. In the blurry picture he had provided, he looked arrogant. His lips were pushed slightly forward in it, his long hair covering half of his face. The image projected a vanity that was excessive even for a selfie; the face in it bluntly told viewers it was too good for them. It was probably right. It was better in this light, less brittle, more human. It looked like less of an object.

His face was angular, his mouth modest. His long, black hair was wet. It fell in waves to his chin; he tucked it behind his ears like tweedy professors tuck pencils.

The man stood in the doorway and smiled at Ilan. The two of them stood roughly the same height. They kept a safe distance away from each other. They didn't shake hands or hug. Instead, they just exchanged smiles. Like they might give a co-worker or a stranger whose eyes he inadvertently caught in the office or on the street.

His shirt was yellow. His underwear was gray. Briefs. Tightly fit to him. Ilan knew from photos that the man had sent what was under the gray cloth.

The man said, "Hello," to them in a slight British accent. Ilan nodded and apologized to him for the delay and for their appearance. They didn't know whether they actually were late. They did know that they looked like shit.

Ilan was led in through a hallway and the living room. They took off their boots near the door without being asked. The apartment was well-kept and decorated with professionally taken photographs of children and paintings of brimming fruit bowls and beaches and olive trees. The paintings were obviously amateur; Ilan assumed that the family had an elderly member who had taken up painting in his retirement. There was a Persian rug and a dark wood piano and dark wood furniture dressed with white doilies and a dark wood grandfather clock with a brass face and dark wood shelves with books in multiple languages and many wood and gold crosses. There were plush couches in mid-century colors: olive and vermilion. It was dimly lit. The windows were open behind white, lace curtains. It was the apartment of someone who had immigrated here, as everyone else had.

Ilan complimented the apartment and said it was "tasteful." After they said it, they realized how condescending it had sounded.

"This is my boyfriend's house. The décor is not my choice, but you're kind to compliment his taste because I hate it." A smile. Two smiles.

The two of them stopped in the kitchen. The man opened the fridge and took out two beers and handed one to them. There was a desiccated peach inside, some sauces, nothing else. Ilan inferred that the boyfriend had been out of town for a while, that the man had the run of the place for a couple of weeks.

Hips against counters, they stood and talked and sipped the canned beer. It was thin tasting. It was the kind of beer that teenagers buy because they don't know better. They were nervous and drank like it. They were almost through the beer in a minute.

Ilan remarked on the crosses. The man shrugged. "They're his, too," he said. "He's like many old and sick people. He likes to pray."

The man asked if Ilan was religious, said it with a kind of dismissive distance. Ilan said they were. Sort of. They didn't say the word "Christian." It would've sounded comical in the context. "I have a weakness for hope," they said instead. "I can't give it up."

The man nodded. Ilan nodded. They both drank.

"So, what were you up to tonight?" the man asked. "You seemed like you were in a rush."

Ilan thought of telling him, thought of saying that this was their last night in the world, their last opportunity to end up in a stranger's apartment. They thought the better of it. "In a way, aren't we all in a rush?" They smiled.

The man didn't respond. He opened the refrigerator door and grabbed two more beers. "Have another," he instructed.

They stood in silence for a moment, again focused nervously on the respective faces of their respective beer cans. Ilan could hear yelling from the street, a higher voice, inflected with booze. They could hear the man breathing. They examined the linoleum floor and ran their fingers through their hair.

"I think we're about done here," the man said, breaking the silence. "Don't you?"

"Sure thing," Ilan replied with a smile. They were finished with the niceties.

The man set down the can, grabbed Ilan's hand, and led them out. Through another hallway lined with photographs and through to a dimly lit bedroom. Inoffensive jazz music played; the lyrics were inaudible but unmistakably foreign. A mirror-faced closet was closed on one wall. On another, a disordered bookshelf with papers and thick volumes of what looked like a set of encyclopedias. A yellow-sheeted mattress sagged on the floor. It was squat. No frame. There was a black-screened television set turned off in the corner, and near it, three large suitcases and several large cardboard boxes sat open on the floor, their contents—clothes and books, mostly— roughly pulled out of them.

Their eyes were still running over the room when the man turned and started kissing them. The man leaned into Ilan and put his hands on their neck. The two mouths were beer-bitter, the two necks sweat-slicked. Ilan still had the half-empty beer can in their hand.

Ilan slid the man's yellow shirt off and tried to catch the rhythm of the kiss, tried to match the other mouth's movements. They opened to it. They let the other tongue have its way. And then they mirrored, matched it.

Ilan was moved to the edge of the bed. The man stood in front of them naked. He'd gotten out of the gray underwear without announcing it. Ilan touched him there, where the fabric had just been, their fingers running through the dense, curly, black hair. Their other hand set the beer can on the side table.

Ilan slumped onto the mattress, which they found was already wet, already sweated into, and unbuttoned and unzipped themselves. The man removed their pants, flung them toward the wall of mirrors. Ilan watched the man's back as their shirt was pulled off, saw the muscles in it move, saw the long line of his spine and the contrapposto hips and the two long, hairy legs, one bent, the other straight. And then the man was on top of them, wet skin on wetter skin, the smell of beer and toothpaste and hair and deodorant and the sweaty sheet and the desert coming in from the window. And then the sight of the man as his mouth moved slowly down Ilan's stomach, the black and the blue in the waves of his hair and the tan of his skin and the red curling letters on his chest and the sinews in his arms and the lighter skin of his hips where the sun hadn't browned him and his long, sloping neck which now seemed to Ilan the most human and the most animal looking thing they'd ever seen.

And Ilan thought of tomorrow and of tonight and all the nights like this that they'd known in their life and all the people who had been with them on beds like this one and the kindness and tenderness they had shown. And they felt the weight of the end of those nights and the importance attached to this one and they were grateful that they were spending it with a man like this. And they looked again at the man's reflection in the mirror and tried to fill their eyes with it, conscious that they would need to rely on the image over and over again in the future. And they thought of a line from Ovid that they remembered from their largely worthless and anachronistic classical education and tied the image to it, hoping that it would anchor everything to something real and memorable: "As she stood before my eyes with raiment cast aside, nowhere over her entire body was there a single blemish. Why should I relate her features one-by-one? Nothing did I see that was not praiseworthy."

TANDEM

Riverside

A young man's body. A man's body. A body. Warmth. A place to hide.

"You shouldn't be embarrassed about your body when you're around me," he said to me in the beginning. He said it to put me in my place, to draw attention to the difference in our age and physical appearance. Like so many things he said then, the childishness of it made me smile. He really did think it would hurt me. He thought that I'd give a shit. He was right, though. I did feel embarrassed about it.

He says different things now. Different things or no things. He has little to say. He is not a child anymore, and he has nothing to be vain about and no one to peacock in front of and no reason to put me in my place. He goes from the window to the bed to the garden to the TV room and watches things happen and is unobserved and unappreciated by the people around him and comes back here to me and resumes being a young man's body. A man's body. A body. A place to hide.

We hide together. He holds me, fucks me, holds me again. He squeezes me, runs his fingers through my hair, and says "I don't want this anymore."

As if there's an alternative.

Before him, there was her. There was sense and order and a house and a regime and a woman to make it all happen, to make me live up to her high standards, to be disappointed when I didn't. There was middle class prosperity and happy parents and good holidays and LA, sprawling and alive. There was an undramatic decade of all that, and then an undramatic, inevitable divorce that neither of us mourned too much.

I knew the day that we signed the papers that I'd regret it. I felt it. I saw what lay ahead— the type of person I had been and would be again without her: inert, dissatisfied, static. I knew she would take six months on her own and then end up someone else's wife and that the marriage would be better than what we'd had, and that the new wife would be kinder, smarter, better looking, more successful. I knew they would have everything: perfect wedding, happy marriage, lovely home, pretty kids, picturesque vacations. I knew I would end up an unfortunate detour en route to the life that she was meant to live. I knew I'd stew and be sad and end up convinced I'd been far happier with her than I'd ever actually been. I knew that I'd do stupid shit.

I signed anyway. I signed because I knew that I was precisely the type of person who signs and regrets. And because there was no way to not end it now. No alternatives.

She unloaded the house. Fast. There was enough interest for that. And she was intent to sell, to liquidate. The house sold for less than what we'd paid for it, but it yielded enough.

Through the lawyers, she offered half. I took $28,000. The estimated amount that I'd put into it in mortgage payments. The minimal amount I could take, without claiming a grace or gallantry that wasn't mine. All the rest was her parents' money. By taking it, I'd have validated her, lived up to her low expectations of me.

I took the few boxes of items that were indisputably mine and went home. Pre-her home. The city was hers, had been hers at the beginning. I left her our usuals, our habitual places, our frequents and familiars, and went home to Riverside.

I moved into a "loft" in Downtown. It was too expensive, but it beat everything else on offer. The last thing I wanted was a long-vacant suburban tract home with extra bedrooms for phantom children. I was willing to pay extra so that I wouldn't have to live in something like that.

A college friend got me an administrative job at UC Riverside. It was a nothing job. It involved few responsibilities and even fewer prospects, but it paid decently and, again, there were no alternatives. The office was on the back end of an old, yellowed, '50s-era building. Inside, in a suite divided into carpeted cubicles, a staff of five typed away our days, a single window looking out over the lawns and lecture halls.

A daily routine emerged. A process driven by muscle memory. A quick spurt of effort in the morning followed by a social media tour through friends and ex-lovers, online shopping, self-improvement considerations, apartment décor, language classes, music classes, mulling over various fitness programs. In the afternoon, a long walk across the lawns and down the street to the Botanical Garden where I identified the spot of maximum seclusion that I'd frequented twenty years before as an undergrad. Two hours later, I'd meander back, package up a report or a letter, walk to the post-box, come back, adjust my belongings, head out. Four p.m. End of day. Await sleep.

At home in the evenings those first few months, the nights passed with a similar numbness. Metronome hours. Books, old films, cleaning, cooking. I shopped compulsively. I took a French history course, aspired to be cultured. I went on long runs, looking like one of those wiry, California granola women in sports bras who expound the virtues of organic deodorant in the line at Sprouts. I drove for hours, down empty side-streets or freeways to Palm Springs or out to Newport, past long vacated houses of childhood friends, former schools, nightspots where I'd had dates fifteen years ago.

Fifty milligrams a day of Paxil prescribed by a mercifully permissive and uninquisitive psychiatrist made it possible. A keen sense that this was as good as it gets made it possible. Booze made it possible.

I took to frequenting the one gay bar in Downtown. Menagerie, where in my college days we would come to consume drag performances and blue drinks and Kylie Minogue. It was the first place where I saw real queer people dance with each other, the first place where I saw them kiss, the first place where I saw their relationships commence and collapse. My senior year, a man was stabbed to death in the back parking lot, one of those not infrequent occasions when a mob of straight young men make their invisible masculinity visible by painting it on the asphalt in blood.

In the years since, like most gay bars, it emptied out, turned half-museum, half-straight dive bar. The drag performers left. The music went standard electronic. Most of the regulars married or moved or died. The bar remained, preserved as a sad, sleepy memorial to the time when it had been necessary. But the booze was cheap, and the smoking patio remained, and the rainbow flag still flew and a dwindling queer contingent—mostly young, mostly seeing the place as quaint and past-tense—still came every now and then.

Two or three nights a week, I would come to get drunk and observe, comfortable in my middle-aged female invisibility. Most nights, I would take a seat outside and empty out three or four full glasses of whatever was on special. The well whiskey sour. The well rum and coke. Two or three hours later, sufficiently loaded, I'd head home to order an enchilada plate from Tio's Tacos and sleep it off.

The night I met him marked maybe the one hundredth reenactment of this routine. It was summer and the bar was half-empty and even sadder and quieter than usual. Alone, I took my vodka and escaped out back to my corner. Around me, a couple of tables full of chatterers went about their work, competing with the indistinct house music. A group of semi-trashed girls in their late girlhood were talking too loudly about the failings of boyfriends, the table top in front of them covered with empty shot glasses. Double-daters were sipping glasses of wine. And a familiar young man, legs crossed in his lap, sat alone in the corner opposite me, his face down in a book.

In a more sexually expressive time, he wouldn't have gone long here without becoming a focal point. Long, dirty blonde hair tied up in a knot on the top of his head. Green-hazel eyes. Sandaled feet with their dusting of blonde hair. Eighties-style athletic shorts up to mid-thigh. The object of objects. A ready-made pin cushion for the eye to puncture.

We met in the French history class that I'd taken months before. He played the class asshole then, disputing the professor's assertions and questions in the condescending way that entitled boys who overestimate their own intelligence and importance do, shouting her down. Everyone in the class, including me, had hated him. Everyone in the class, including me, had let our eyes run over his body, nonetheless.

On the uncounted tenth or twentieth glance in his direction, I noticed his seat empty. I lit another cigarette and contented myself with eavesdropping on the drunk girls. I resolved to get up for another drink when he reappeared around the corner.

"I figured that, if you're going to stare at me all night, we might as well exchange names." He smiled, two cups of clear liquid in his hands. "I'm Kevin, and I come bearing gifts."

He handed me the cup and fell into the bench seat next to me.

Conversation revealed that he played the same character outside the classroom as he did inside it. He asked me why I was here all alone, whether my girlfriend was with me, and sorry, but he had just assumed I was a lesbian given the way that I dressed and talked. "But now I get more of a bi vibe off of you." The charmer.

I asked him why he was here alone. "You looking to pick someone up?"

"No," he said. "I just like the eyes every now and then and the free drinks."

He liked to hear himself talk. He liked to say stupid things. The strangeness of a woman my age and boy his age having this conversation. The remarkable fact that a woman my age would be attending classes with undergraduates, still caring. The ease with which he could get us both free drinks since the bartender was into him. How disturbing and slightly disgusting he found attention from gay guys, but how he exploited it.

When he stopped for breath, I pulled two cigarettes from the box and offered one to him. "Turkish delight for the little prince?" He laughed and refused, so I lit both and alternated between them until the nicotine gave me a stomach ache.

He went on a tear for a half an hour or so talking nonsense. His words were a rehash of everything current on right-wing cable television, all the bile and bias. I could tell he believed very little of it, that he was just trying to get a rise out of me. Observing the show high up in the rear mezzanine, I ran out of booze.

"Drink's empty." I announced. "What's say you use your extensive connections to fill it up again, ok?" He smiled at me and obeyed.

While he attended to the refill, I considered making an escape, walking the three blocks back to the apartment, turning on some home renovation show, acting my age, falling asleep. Another hour of this would accomplish what? Entertainment? Stress relief? Free drinks?

There was another possible outcome. The kid's mouth on mine, his patchy, blonde facial hair scratching my cheek, his hands on my hips, and his fingers inside me, his tongue sliding down my neck and breasts and stomach and pubic hair, my fingers holding his head there. The image lingered for a few moments. I made myself laugh at it.

He came back into view carrying a cardboard coffee carrier with four drinks wedged into it. I laughed out loud.

"Nice to know you at least have one legit good idea in that head of yours." He gave me a half-smile before launching into another half hour-long harangue.

We got drunk together. We got drunk, and he talked, and I looked at him and kept drinking. His voice came in and came out. His voice and his image in various states of undress. I forgot to make myself laugh at it.

We left the bar together around midnight. He had exhausted both of us. We had both passed from drunk to borderline incoherent. The people around us had left. It was late.

I didn't invite him to come with me, but he came anyway. We walked in silence back to my apartment. It was hot and sticky. Night insects were chirping. The sidewalks were empty. There were few cars on the road. He walked far ahead of me and then dropped behind and then came up right beside me, coming far too close, seeming much drunker than he had before.

We arrived at my building. He shifted nervously, quiet and small and even younger-looking. I wished him a quick good night and then—for a reason known only to the drunk version of me—patted him lightly on the head and went inside.

Ten minutes later, the front door buzzer sounded. I considered briefly—something— and then pressed the button to admit him, going out into the hall to wait. Minutes passed, and then I watched him appear, stride down the hallway, slide past me, and walk into the apartment. I followed him.

From the kitchen, I watched him pace, knit his hands together, sit on the floor, slide off his sandals, unbutton his shirt. I watched him remove the tie from his hair and pull the shirt off and unbutton his shorts. I watched him pull the shorts and the underwear off and let them fall to the ground.

I watched him stand there naked and then walk over to the bathroom and shut and lock the door. I watched and said nothing and then grabbed a bottle of scotch out of the liquor cabinet and drank from it.

I looked at the bathroom door, listening as he shuffled things around and flushed the toilet and turned on the shower. I realized that I needed to be drunker than this, or someplace other than this, or to slip on a different persona. I needed to have intended him to end up here, to be the kind of woman who invites young men home and then fucks them. Fucks them. Which would require me to want to fuck him. Which I assumed I didn't. Which I hoped I didn't.

He finally came out of the bathroom, a towel wrapped around his waist, bare chested. My towel, wet and dripping on the concrete.

"What the fuck are you doing?" No response.

I laughed. "What exactly do you want to come out of this?" No response.

I got up, walked around him, grabbed a bathrobe from behind the bathroom door, and handed it to him. "You wear this, ok? You wear it and you don't take it off. Or you can put your fucking clothes back on."

He stayed the night on the couch. In my bedroom, my door locked, I was unable to sleep. I got up and walked out to the living room and watched him for a bit, looked at his bare legs hanging over the edge of the couch. I tried to figure out if I had willed this to happen, if I had made it occur. I wondered what Nicole would've said about it, how evident her disappointment would be, how fully it would fit her image of me. I measured how distant I was from who I had been, how far from the sense and stability that she created for us. Together, no drunk, racist, sexist, fucked up boys had invited themselves in at midnight. No drunk, stupid me had buzzed them up.

He left in the early morning sometime, in the three-hour window between the time that I fell asleep and the time that

I was jarred awake by a dream in which he was naked in bed with me and tying me up. The robe and the blanket lay neatly folded on the couch along with a scribbled note with his phone number on it. "Sorry for the confusion. Kevin." I read it and laughed and poured myself another scotch.

I took a long break from drinking. I tried to take a real interest in work, tried to clean myself up. I went on a proper date for the first time since the divorce with an architect from Pomona who spent most of dinner talking about her ex-wife and her son. I exercised. I went to church. I made and stuck to a monthly budget. I tried to do all the things Nicole used to do, all the things I hated doing with her.

After a little more than a month of this, he came back. He showed up at the apartment at 11:35 on a weeknight, buzzed half a dozen times, rang the apartment phone, asked to come up. I hung up. And then three days later, the same thing, closing in on midnight, trying to wear me down through sheer, dedicated annoyance. His liquid courage hour, I assumed. He tried email and social media, asking to meet so he could apologize. For a week, he became a real, true bore. And then, after a couple of days, nothing. Boy appears. Boy disappears.

The invitation came soon after. The Save-the-Date printed on recycled cardboard. A plantable card, it said on the back. Seed paper. Grows wildflowers. It would happen in Santa Barbara in June. The fiancée's name was Jennifer. She was an anesthesiologist from Carpinteria, tall and blonde and browned and good-looking in that Santa Barbara way. She was young, accomplished, stable, good. She was, as I had anticipated, a definite trade up.

I called him up that night, after halving a bottle of Triple Sec, the last remnants of the liquor cabinet.

He arrived half an hour later, buzzed up and straight to the door and the lights turned off and the curtains drawn and the noise of passing cars breezing through the open windows.

Sex occurred. It happened. It was forgettable, disembodied, a series of automatic motions in which convention overruled the mind, like laughing at a bad joke or nodding at an irrelevant observation. Out of a lifetime's understanding of what it is, you do it. What it consists of: move this like that, yield in this way at this time, make that noise, breathe, shut your eyes, kiss him, reciprocate the kiss he offers you, cover his penis with your mouth, count the sucks up to 50, kiss him again, be silent, let him finish. The body does it on its own. The mind does different things, says different things. This is why you fail, it says. This is why the marriage failed, why most marriages fail, when one of the two is less than, upsetting the symmetry, doing stupid things out of boredom just to see whether they'll wreck everything.

Absent. Absent from the bed. Absent from the room. Absent from this boy, whoever he was, whatever ridiculous, nonsensical, doomed thing he wanted. Absent from myself, from the moving and the moaning, from envying wedding plans and Pinterest boards and plantable Save-the-Dates.

When he finished, he lay flat on top of me, silent, his face turned away toward the wall, mine in the opposite direction. Our bodies disengaged each other, cold and damp and heavy, his head on my shoulder.

It became habitual. Twice or three times weekly, I'd text him. "Tonight?" or "This evening" or "Let me know about later." He'd arrive late. He'd buzz, come up, turn off the lights, undress himself. I'd be moved to the bed. I'd be undressed. I'd have sex, be had sex with, become the object of sex. He'd finish. I'd sometimes pretend to finish. We'd lay next to each other. I'd fall asleep. He'd let himself out.

After he was done and before he left, we talked. We were candid, intimate, now that we knew and didn't know each other so well.

He was younger even than he looked, barely nineteen. He was an only son, with all the attendant expectations and entitlements. He grew up in Apple Valley, into a hard-right, talk-radio family: sisters, dead mother, drunk father, stern grandparents who housed but didn't care for them. He attempted suicide at 13, been committed to a care facility where he'd lived and been educated until he was 18. They let him out for college with his grandparents' permission. He hadn't done well. He had no idea where life would lead him but was justifiably pessimistic about his prospects, about the slim likelihood of finding a job, about the even slimmer likelihood that he would find something he liked. He hated going home, hated his roommates, was glad the house where he lived was big enough to avoid them. He spent most of his days alone. At the movies, at cafes, at hookah bars where he'd bring a book with him and sit and smoke for hours.

In his one year of independence, he had no proper relationships and just a handful of real dates. Instead, he'd had sex. Frequently, he indicated. With whoever he found online, which was frequently older women in LA and Orange County and San Diego who he'd drive fifty or a hundred miles to see and then never see again. Once, he'd met a woman in her 50s from Chicago who was visiting Las Vegas on a business trip. He drove all night to see her, stayed for two hours, drove the four hours back, never contacted her again. In the facility, he'd "messed around" with other boys. He didn't want to say anything about it.

He did not discuss what occurred between us. I did not bring the subject up, rarely brought any subjects up. In the dark, the confessional screen between us, he divulged without prompting. In the dark, I offered occasional comment. In the dark, he prompted me to divulge. In the dark, I answered what he asked.

He was not exceptionally affectionate. Not exceptionally cold, either. The body that moved over me did so with a certain gentility but without any indication that it considered the body that it moved over special. It was efficient and business-like. Afterward, on top of or against me, it didn't cling or comfort. It lay, a simple fact. Proximate. He was not exceptionally drunk on desire. He rarely made any noises indicating pleasure. Breaths caught, sighs came, undramatic and emotionless. Muffled, in a way, as though he didn't want to disturb me.

I remember he moved a mirror in front of the bed once and fucked me in front of it. I remember he didn't ask my permission to move it. I remember he just came in and undressed and took it out of the hallway and put it against the wall in the bedroom.

After he was done, he asked me why I'd kept my eyes closed the entire time, why I hadn't looked even once.

"You don't understand," I said. "I prefer to not be here when it happens."

Winter came and went, first wet, then colder than it had been in two decades, then scorching hot, then cold again. Brown fields went green from rain then so brown that wildfires broke out in March. The news was full of disasters: a chain of attacks on airports and train stations, a string of school shootings with increasing death tolls, mosques bombed, immigrants deported, workers laid off, suburban housing developments set on fire in Henderson and San Antonio and Tampa. The rhythms of life—already upset, already disturbed by the era and the mood, by politics and the economy—deteriorated even further. Already dwindling crowds in stores, on streets, and on sidewalks became even sparser. On campus, faculty and students thinned out, the lawns quiet as kids went home to the protection of their parents.

Things declined. The bar closed. The other apartments in the complex all seemed to be up for sale. At work, shifts were cut, faculty were furloughed. Retirement came for three of us. My shift was cut in spring, from 40 to 20 hours.

Life, its few remaining threads, simplified. Money fell away, though the rent and gas and booze and other, minor expenses fell with it, cushioning the impact. Remaining friends went without explanation, off to find something else someplace else. Family remained dead, remote, forgotten. Alone, he came and went and came and went as before.

As scheduled, they married. A flood of pictures, a flood of faces on social media. Strangers now, well and truly. Wrapped up in lives that were ever stranger, ever more foreign. On the other side of the glass, people still danced in floral dream-worlds, still wrapped themselves in linens and silks as though they were safe, still sipped real champagne from cut crystal, still performed their love for one another in front of hundreds who found the performance credible and important.

He was left. He was all that was left.

"Why do you come here every night?" I asked him once, after we'd finished.

"Why not?" he answered. "What else have I got to do?"

"Well, maybe you should try to find something."

"Maybe one day," he said. "When I get tired of this."

Passing into his twenties, he thickened. His arms and chest broadened and grew hairy. He aged five years in a few months. He rushed into a body that should've grown up gradually. The voice, already deep, grew deeper, the speech more taciturn. He was less intent on proving things. He was sadder, as everyone seemed to be.

One night that summer, without discussion, he stayed the night for the first time. One Saturday, after the usual, after the barest, briefest exchange of words, I awoke around

4 a.m. to him still next to me, this heavy thing, this mass, his arm hanging heavy over me. For hours, I was pinned there, examining the walls, his breath steaming up the back of my neck, his sweat dripping on my skin. I couldn't sleep with him on me, by me, over me. He made it hard to breathe.

When he finally woke, there were no words. And then he was up, exposed in the daylight, the hard, heavy, hairy body in view as he went to the toilet and came back and slid on his jeans in front of me, buttoned the shirt, put on his shoes. And then, again for the first time, he leaned in for a kiss and looked at me. "I don't want this anymore," he said, and then turned and left.

Days passed. I texted, with no response. And again and again. "Are you all right?" "Are you hurt?"

I called, with no response. Online, I searched and found that the usual profiles and markers had been removed, the pictures gone. I searched the campus buildings and departments that I assumed he frequented, the complex where I remember he lived, the hangouts he'd mentioned. Nothing.

His grandparents were easy enough to find. Listed online, behind an easily breachable paywall— the number, address, ages, media profiles, employment history. A call and I met a woman's rough, smoker's voice. A serviceable lie came out of my mouth. I was his professor, checking to see why he hadn't been in class in a week. The voice choked out an abrupt reply. "Whoever you are, you take this up with the facility. He's over there for good now."

"You had no right to commit him," I yelled into the phone.

"Lady, he committed himself," she replied.

It wasn't hard to check in. They accepted anyone and were especially happy to admit those who did so willingly. The day

I signed the papers—admittance day, they called it—I knew I'd regret it. I signed anyway.

There didn't seem to be any alternatives. There was only him. A young man's body. Warmth. Shelter. A place to hide. Together. In tandem.

He resented it initially. I was embarrassed initially. Embarrassed to have revealed so much of myself. In time, those feelings waned. In time, we both stopped caring enough to feel them.

CROWN ROYAL

San Dimas

The last bottle June drank was a favorite. Crown Royal. She wasn't much for experimentation these days. She was into things she knew. Comfort.

Crown Royal comforted. It was most of the previous thirty years' evenings. Filling a third of a big plastic soda cup. Opaque, so the kids wouldn't start wondering. Mixed in with Diet Coke because she'd never been too imaginative and because it seemed healthier and lasted longer that way. She'd have it after dinner. Sip on it for a couple of hours. She had enough self-control for that. Nothing too abrupt or alarming. Just a respectable, gradual slump over the course of an hour or two with the evening news. And then off to bed at eight and asleep instantly with its assistance.

It had a decent taste for the price. She could always taste it, even with the Diet Coke. Could tell the difference even with the soda. Which is why she'd never done Canadian Club. The cheap shit. At the very least, it had to be Crown Royal. In better times, XR or Stranahan's. That put a smile on your face. That made you feel good about life. But this was sufficient. It did the job. It was the best she could justify in reduced circumstances. Two-liter bottles of it took care of $60 of the remaining $11,000 and change that made up her savings.

She poured it straight. No need anymore to be coy. No need to conceal from the ex-wife or the kids. The ex-wife had a new wife. She still had power of attorney, though. June had never gotten around to revoking that. She had access to the accounts. She shopped for June at Costco. She occasionally still came around to threaten her, to tell her she'd check her into a care facility if she didn't clean herself up and get to a meeting. She knew she was probably stealing shit. Good for her, the bitch.

As for the kids, that was done, too. They were off doing their own thing. One lived in LA and taught high school and wrote and didn't come around unless he needed money. Another lived in Denver and had a husband and a couple of kids of her own. The last lived in his car in Palmdale. June hadn't spoken to any of them in more than a year.

She took it in a cognac glass. That was a phase. When the business was good. Cognac and cigars. Not because she liked them but because she worked with men and because she wanted to mess with them, wanted to toy with their notions of what bosses, male bosses act like. They drink cognac and smoke cigars to prove to themselves they're good. They've made it. Someplace. Someplace with fuckers in beige shorts and polo shirts. Cognac and cigars because that's the milieu. June didn't have a milieu now. Never had. She'd always been a cigarettes and Crown Royal sort of person. But the cognac glass was clean, so why not drink out of a little bulb?

She sipped it and hobbled over toward the patio, holding the crutch with her free arm. She was still clunky with it, but she managed. She got out the door, sat down on the patio, sipped, and lit up. B&H 100s. The Crown Royal of cigarettes. Things went together.

It was early evening. As usual, the sky above San Dimas was full of smog. It blew here from LA and the mountains caught it. She could see out over the valley, all the way to Pasadena. She could see the Forest Lawn mausoleum where her father and mother were interred. The traffic was heavy. The breeze was cool. The sunset was dirty and brilliant. Apocalypse red.

She wasn't fucking around anymore, and so she finished the first glass in three minutes, the first cigarette in two. She staggered up and managed three or four steps forward toward the house, just enough to grab the bottle, which she'd set on the living room couch. She knocked over the lamp in the process, but it was tough. The ceramic vase-looking part of it didn't break. She wouldn't have cared if it had.

Another full glass, another cigarette. She was aware that life is just a list of things you've consumed. It didn't depress her. She was happy to add two more items. She had her phone with her and put on some music. Comfort, again. Mel McDaniel. "Louisiana Saturday Night." Just a bunch of peckerwood stereotypes in a smoker's voice. Line dance music. Dumb as all hell. But comforting. She'd danced to it with her first wife at The Palms in West Hollywood thirty years ago, back when lesbian bars were still a thing.

The night was down. Down on the yard and the patio and the house, with all the lights off. She wasn't in the mood to get up and turn them on. No matter. She had enough light on the phone and the end of the cigarette. And it was pleasant. The darkness obscured, wiped away. Wiped away the cast. Wiped away her totaled pickup, its jagged nose sticking out of the carport. Wiped away her wrinkled brown hands and the emptying bottle.

She poured more. Splashed most of it on the glass tabletop. It was fully dark now. Her phone lit up with a text from her sister. "Happy Birthday, Junebug!" She raised a glass to that. Fifty-fucking-eight. Going on sixty-fucking-eight from the look of her. But above ground for the moment, and so ok. She downed the glass.

The bottle was empty. She'd made short work of it. "Well, that's it," she said to herself, but then rethought it. Gave herself license to open another. And that is why, when her ex-wife came to check on her three days later, she found June's body on the track of the sliding glass door, with the front end of her in the living room pointing toward a full bottle of Crown Royal in the kitchen and her legs pointing toward an empty one on the patio table.

31

CASUAL

Ontario

I remembered him in mid-afternoon, after my mother
finished questions and answers over coffee and sugar-free
wafers, with the dog comatose on the coach in its cancer meds
stupor. I meant to spend two or three hours with her between
the end of the conference and a string of area inspections, a
sort of goodbye for the dog, whose tumors were now fully
visible, little rosettes peeking out through the fur. I stayed
only an hour and ten now that the narcoleptic skeleton on the
couch bore little resemblance to the dog I grew up with.

Down the 60 on the way toward his place, I gurgled
sparkling water to mute the sour coffee breath. A couple years
before, I'd have fished out a travel toothbrush in the glove
box and scraped off my tongue and spat into coffee cups and
maybe stopped to buy Listerine. But there was less to prove
these days.

I unblocked the contact on my phone and then texted to
see if he was still there on the cul-de-sac where he was when I
last checked nine months prior. I loitered a bit at a gas station
down the street waiting for a response, putting the rental
through a coin op car wash and then browsing in the nuts and
chips, until a "HEY STRANGER" came back at me from the
ether. And we were off.

These meetups always began this way, had for the past
fifteen years—never arranged, never belabored, just a text
from nowhere and a hope that it would be received in time. I'd
had about a 50% success rate. If he were in a relationship or
out of town or not in proximity to his cell phone in the thirty-
minute gap between the time that I texted and the time that I
headed back, it was a no go. The rest of the time, it was "HEY
STRANGER" and then up the hill in fifteen.

"I'll have to shower. Been sunbathing in the backyard." In the 104-degree heat, in the oven breeze. I'd have reddened, peeled, burned; his skin took the sun and translated it into gold, into fullness, into warmth. "Wait for me just a bit."

I sped up the hill, past the old rodeo grounds, past empty, trash-strewn plots of land, railroad tracks, and an elementary school with a busted LED sign announcing the beginning of summer break two years ago. And then through ranch houses and Spanish villas and up to the familiar squat brown bungalow with its front lawn torn up.

My phone was dead, and his two roommates were doing yard work in the front. They were a couple, bearish and rumpled and in their 50s. I parked and cracked a book open; he'd come and get me when they were gone. That was the drill; they go out, I'd be let in, or else they wouldn't go out and I'd be snuck past without acknowledgement. "I prefer not to introduce my tricks," he said last time with a wink.

Two days before Christmas last year, I texted on getting in from New York for a weekend of inspections after checking in to Doubletree near the airport. We emptied a bottle of tequila in his backyard, chatted and shared a smoke in front of the firepit, and then spent the night together, lazily moving through the motions. It was crossfaded sex, lots of ridiculous, slow licking and breaks for laughter. And then we watched *Family Guy* and fell asleep. I left in the early morning without saying goodbye.

I'd not mind repeating that episode. He kept me waiting for it for half an hour. Finally, the roommates piled into the helm of a pick-up truck 5 feet off the ground and disappeared down the road. Five minutes later, he tapped on the window in a wife-beater and basketball shorts, bare feet on the sidewalk. Sweat droplets collected on his shoulders, shone gray through the thin white cloth on his torso. He smiled lazily, that half-high grin that he always wore.

I opened the door and slid out, scalding my thighs on the super-heated car seat. He stood about a head taller, had maybe 70 pounds on me, all visible in the arms and chest and thighs and in his thick, sinuous, veiny neck. I put my hand around that neck and rubbed it and pulled him in for a brief kiss. I felt his arms wrap around me and his coarse, blistered hands slide under my shirt.

Shades still on, I opened my eyes and examined his face and felt myself harden. It was still there, what had drawn me to him so long ago. There was still softness in the lips and vividness in the green eyes and waviness in the hair, even if it had thinned and greyed in the temples.

He led me into the house. As ever, it was a mess—a dingy, popcorn-ceilinged, mid-'70s mess. Brown, shag carpet. Thick, woolen drapes. He'd lived here for the last ten years in a child-sized room that always stank of pot. This time was no different. The volcano in the corner still had gray smoke lingering in the bag and a graveyard of tokes lay in the belly of a murder-weapon weight crystal ashtray. A mound of dirty shirts and underwear lay on the bed and the floor.

He'd lit a fat, peach-colored candle on the dresser, which let off a vaguely floral smell. It mixed with the scent of weed and the dirty clothes. Mingled together, it was sweet and musky and chemical, one of those smells that you encounter on subways and find both unappealing and slightly erotic. "Mmmm... So romantic," I needled him.

He disappeared for a few minutes and then came back with two mugs full of coconut-flavored rum. I gulped down half of mine and then lay down on the bed on top of the pile of dirty clothes and pressed my face into them and inhaled.

By the time I turned back, he had already stripped down to just a jockstrap. He now pulled that down and let it fall at his feet. Naked but for his socks, he lay down next to me.

The eyes and fingers always had first dibs, always had the privilege of examining, initiating. They ran over him, reminding me of the terrain. Giant arms and shoulders, the skin turned coarse and freckled by the sun. Swollen chest and the pillow of the red, almond-shaped scar on his breastbone.

Hard, shaved stomach. Stretch marks, ghostly white. At the hips, sharp angled bones intruding. Shaved pubic hair and thick, unshaven black hair on his thighs and calves, a few rogue strands of gray visible.

Fifteen years earlier, this body had shocked me, even shamed me. There was something incongruous about it, putting my limbs in proximity to it, as though I were made of the same material. I would ask for the lights to be turned off. I would pull parts of myself away, shroud them up in the sheets, not necessarily afraid that he would be disappointed, but acutely conscious of the differences between him and me, the distance between ideal and reality.

We'd met on an app. I'd put up a profile after a breakup, the first breakup, when the best alternative to repeatedly drunk texting the guy seemed to be to instantly and continuously replacing him. I filled that profile with lies and exaggeration.

His message stood out in the pile of dick pics and orgy invitations. He introduced himself: thirty-three, a psychiatrist, local. Complimented me. Said he'd like to take me out for drinks. I was two weeks shy of 21 but agreed to the day after my birthday, lying that I'd be out of town for a bit at a conference. In the meantime, we agreed to talk on the phone.

I took the call around midnight on a Saturday, puffing Pall-Malls in the alley outside my apartment. Downed a tumbler of Popov before to calm the nerves, the better to play at carelessness. We talked for three hours as I emptied the rest of the box of cigarettes, exchanging lives, talking guys and vacations and booze and my studies and his work. Slicked by exaggeration, I made every attempt to stretch out to a full adult length, to make the age difference between us less obscenely wide. For his part, he didn't make any reference to it whatsoever.

We met a few days later at a dive bar in Downtown Riverside. He was breezy and comfortable and good-looking. Tight sweater, tight jeans, all black, like he'd just broken out of a BMW ad. I was dumpy and dressed down in ill-fitting, clearance rack clothes that hung from my body in the typical rumpled college student way. I felt and looked like a child, unattractive, uncomfortable, incomplete.

In spite of this, I performed all right. The conversation was easy, and the flirting was natural. I got in front of "the age thing," asked him brusquely if he made a habit of going out with college students. He asked, with equal abruptness, if I had a habit of going out with older men. "Not really, just tends to come out that way." Not true in those days, though it would be in the months and years afterward.

I ordered Black Label and drank it like it was a rum and coke. He ordered a rum and coke and drank it like it was Black Label. We talked about his recent breakup and about mine. I stretched four months to two years, revised the mess of a nineteen-year-old boy at the other end of that into a 25-five-year old graduate student with whom I'd shared an apartment and dogs. I kept my mind out of where it naturally tended, out of consideration of the body in front of me, out of consideration of the way it might feel and smell and taste.

At the end of the night, three drinks in the can, my tongue and my judgment sufficiently loosened up, we left. He asked to walk me to my car, a ramshackle, dent-encrusted, shamefully decrepit Cadillac Deville that had previously been owned by my grandparents. I made a slurred excuse that I had taken the train.

And so, he pulled me in and kissed me good night in the bar parking lot. After twenty years of locked hips and intricate lies, after a year of trying to make myself comfortable being "public" with what I'd never anticipated being public, panic shot through me. I imagined angry male eyes looking out from angry male faces. My mind ran through news stories of couples getting jumped for much less.

He lingered for a moment, my eyes on his eyelids, before pulling back. And then, a faint smirk and a whispered "Can

I see you again?" The best of signs. I caught my breath and silently nodded back, mirroring the half-smile.

I walked away, through a cloud of clove-scented smoke surrounding a small crowd of young, presumably drunken men on motorcycles. I was a stew of dreaminess and whiskey and anxiety that we'd been seen and dissatisfaction that I'd not really enjoyed the kiss that I'd imagined for two weeks.

Drunkenness overwhelming judgment, I turned back from the edge of the parking lot and caught sight of the broad back rounding the corner. I jogged toward it.

In three minutes, I undid the careful façade that I'd constructed in the previous two weeks. Over the bones of the mature, unearnest man I pretended to be, I unmasked the bumbling, inexperienced, horny little boy I was. I stammered out an over-eager explanation. I'd had such a fantastic night and I'd been looking forward to it for so many days, thinking about it for so long, that I didn't want to say goodnight, and couldn't we go someplace and keep the conversation going, keep getting to know each other, and couldn't that someplace be his place?

We walked to his car, one of those high-perched Ford Tonka trucks that men like because they look like they just emerged full size from a Happy Meal box. I fumbled to open the door before he unlocked it, and we danced awkwardly, my hand two steps ahead of the beeper. Again, over-heated and over-eager, with desperation in spades. We sped down the freeway to his apartment, my eyes out the window, his on the road, and nothing between us but the transaction to come.

The apartment was pure single man. Messy, incompletely furnished. Clothes on the floor. A mattress with no frame. A bathroom with a counter covered with toothpaste tubes and pill bottles and used Q-tips.

I disappeared into it to examine the goods one more time before he did, to psych myself up. Orifice washing ensued, ablutions performed. And then at it with as much élan as I had liquor in my bloodstream.

Self-conscious movements, self-conscious words. He looked and listened, distant, unmoved. He seemed bored of it all, the familiar act, the procedural. Little more than hand washing or paying bills.

Later, sobering up, the lights and our clothes back on and all my nervousness replaced by the overwhelming urge to go home and his eyes on his phone, scrolling through images of other men, it occurred to me that I'd established this as the pattern. The exposition had been cut short, the payoff delivered prematurely, and all possible mysteries let out of their little boxes. And so, I had nothing to lose, now that we would never go beyond this.

"You're not a psychiatrist, are you?" I asked.

"I'm a middle school counselor," he replied.

"Well... we know who we are now."

"Yup. Not that that matters all that much."

And it was still that. A decade on, with gray creeping into his sideburns and wrinkles coming in around my eyes, with that first exchange joined by a dozen more. Months, years between meetings, all stolen days at the edge of things that really mattered. Blocking phone numbers to prevent embarrassing texts. Forgetting last names and details, inquiring after mothers and fathers who had died years before. And yet, comfortably coming again to meet and perform this ritual. Through upward tongues and hands and legs that closed on hips just so readily. Through blankets and sheets, tossing aside pillows, pulling aside clothes that eagerly separated from skin. And then smells and tastes and bodily geographies that perfectly matched up with all the memories of all the times before.

We finished. Three hours later, with the sun going down and a warm breeze in the air, I stepped out onto the lawn. Naked from the waist up and barefoot, broad arms pinning me to his chest, he kissed the back of my neck and whispered "'Til next time" in my ear. I gave a "yup" in response. Down the lawn and into the car, not turning back to wave goodbye, the usual timeline began.

I'd fly home. Days would go by. I'd maybe think of him for a while, spend time obsessing over pictures of him found online. Imagine those hours, replay them in the shower or on my afternoon commute, miming moments, conjuring up scents and tastes. After a couple of glasses of wine, maybe text him that I'd thought of him, thought of that afternoon, and then playact romance for a few days until the thread went silent. And then, back into the world, until six months or a year and a reason to come back.

The next day, clock-punching costume on, I headed out to a full day of meetings and inspections. A random sampling of centers in the area, as always, with the usual protocol: check the books, view a few rooms, meet with the management, draft recommendations, move on to the next. There were almost always the same findings: too many unnecessary extravagances, inefficient use of space, too many hours assigned to staff, over-utilization of medical personnel, insufficient attention to providing services in line with the residents' packages, redundancies. Always redundancies regardless of whether the center was premium or basic, regardless of whether it was designed for the terminally ill and aged or the idle young.

Around four, I pulled up to the Sunrise, a run-down, low-budget, basic facility we operated in Rialto. The last of the day. One hundred seventy-six beds in an old industrial building previously used as a bottling plant. Mostly retirees but with a few teenagers in a separate wing that operated under the name "Ventana" and was chiefly distinguished by a full-service online educational program that we offered at a premium of $12,000 a year. New management had come in at the end of the last fiscal year, reorganized, taken on implementing most of the recommendations that we'd offered at the end of the last inspection: reductions in force, streamlining program offerings and services, drawing greater distinctions between packages, adding new security protocols and transitioning out more senior staff to cut overhead. After an encouraging conversation with the management, I moved on to tour the suites and wards. Standard procedure, to see that words matched up with practices.

Completing my notes as I did the walk through, I caught sight of him, hunched over an old woman's bed in one of the quadruple occupancy rooms. Only visible from the back, but the same unmistakable shape I'd seen from all possible angles for fifteen years. He was in the full work get up, polo shirt and tight slacks. As handsome, as desire-inducing as ever.

I paused for a moment, imagining him turning around. I saw his eyes meet mine. I saw the familiar smile on his face and maybe a bit of feigned bashfulness. I considered the face that I would wear to meet him, the smirk, the customary "Hey, mister." I saw the possibility of a rare round two before my flight later that day.

I stood and looked for a moment longer and then headed back into the management office to finish my report.

OUT OF MIND

Thessaloniki, Greece

She asked, for the third or fourth time that week, whether he would be able to make it out next month. "You need to be there when we have the conversation with her about going into care," she wrote. "Please."

She was, as she almost always was, right. She was, as she almost always was, much less angry with him than she should be. She was incapable of holding anger for a long time. Unique among older siblings, she had always been kind, patient, even nurturing. She grew into a woman defined by those traits. Like many women, her virtues earned her additional burdens and responsibilities. Among these was the care of a dying sixty-seven-year-old woman with no family and few friends. Their mother.

There were three messages from her. He had ignored them all for days and now answered them, writing that he was sorry, but he'd been busy with the conference; he hadn't had a chance to be on his phone. Even though that's the only place he'd been. That's where his eyes had been glued all the time. There was no legitimate reason why he couldn't have answered immediately; he would have if there had been a man or a job offer on the other end of the messages. There was no legitimate reason, too, why he couldn't make it to Temecula next month to be present when they told their mother that they thought she should stop resisting the inevitable.

And it was inevitable. It was long past inevitable. Pancreatic cancer. A six percent survival rate. And hers, so far advanced, caught so late. With Medicare. She was not in the six percent. She would not stand in their triumphant company. She was in the ninety-four percent. She'd join their ranks, the non-elect, the unblessed, soon. Soon. Undefined. Hanging from a thin wire overhead. A hand would move to cut it in its own time and not bother to let anyone know in advance.

He felt guilty thinking about her, and so he tried to avoid the subject, and this avoidance inspired even more guilt, which inspired even more avoidance. It was deserved guilt. It was well-earned. The guilt that comes, justly, from neglect and selfishness. Ignoring texts from your mother while you look at strangers' nudes on a sex app. Putting yourself, your own comfort, your own well-being, ahead of others who deserve your attention and care. Who've put in the deposit early to receive it later. She put in her deposit, earned it and then some.

She's an ideal American mother. She's a woman who never asks for anything, who never complains or demands or seeks out attention or advertises her goodness. She gets nothing for this. She's a woman who is always treated badly, who is always an afterthought, and never is rude about it, never makes the people who treat her like shit self-conscious about the way they act. That would be rude, she reasons. That would be unkind.

She cleans hotel rooms for forty years. Gets treated like what she is, like the help. Treated like trash. On a good day, she's invisible. No one acknowledges her presence. No one says good morning. No one holds the door for her as she wheels the cleaning cart down the hall. On a bad day, a naked man lying in wait trying to grab hold of her, needles and shit on the floor that she has to pick up and scrub out, families yelling at her and calling the management to say that she didn't provide enough of this or enough of that. She always apologizes. A man tries to rape her and complains to the hotel manager and he gets an apology because he's the guest, and the hotel needs him to lose at craps and come back.

For forty years, she goes to work in this environment, where gropes earn smiles. She gets paid shit for it. It's still enough to buy a house, though, because she denies herself everything and because it's Vegas in the '80s.

She does the American Dream. She has a little bungalow on a street full of other little houses that are owned by hotel service workers. The cost of the air conditioning is almost as much as the mortgage payment. She marries a man who hits her and endures it for a decade without complaint. She has two children with him. In the divorce, she holds the child support over his head, and he drops his plans to go after the house.

The kids and the house cost her everything. She gets her clothes at the Goodwill. She wears her uniform dress, without the apron, on special occasions. She doesn't even have a car. There's no car in the driveway until she dips into the savings to buy them cars in high school. When it's 115 degrees outside, she walks and takes the bus. She does this until his sister gives her old Chrysler to her for a 55th birthday present. At sixty-seven, gray-haired and weighing 90 pounds, with a body full of tumors and poisons, she's driving a 25-year old Concorde with ripped upholstery and an air conditioner that only works half the time.

She sinks everything into the kids. They get the best. The clothes they wear are new and they have all the things they need for school. Daycare in between. Four thousand dollars a year of daycare. She finds the money for school trips and summer enrichment programs. She pays to have her daughter take summer classes at UNLV and for her son to spend a summer interning for Amnesty International in New York. They never understand how. She just digs it up. She finds a way on an annual salary of $33,000 a year.

From the time they are conscious of others, the children dismiss her. They are embarrassed of her. She is too low for them. She represents a class of people they instinctually don't want to belong to and a place that they wish they hadn't come from.

This non-city city, this low place, where culture consists of Debbie Reynolds singing "Tammy" and Rich Little's Reagan impersonation. This place that is all tits and white tigers and cocaine overdoses and feathers and imploding hotels and housewives piling all-you-can-eat crab legs onto filet mignon. Abominable people giving themselves permission to act even more abominably. As if they needed a vacation to bloat themselves on greed, to fill their minds and suitcases with shit, to empty their pockets and their balls. As if they didn't already do that every day of the week in every part of the country. As if that weren't the purpose of America, its poisoned blood.

Her children hate this place, what it means. They hate her for getting its stink out of the carpet. They shame and casually ridicule her for her vocabulary and her behavior.

She talks too loudly and calls the waitress "honey." She doesn't know who the Secretary of State is. She always confuses "your" and "you're." Her eyeshadow is bubblegum pink. It's dollar store makeup. It's cheap. In public, they can't not see her as a woman who wears an apron and scrubs bile out of bed sheets. She has no education. Her knowledge of the world extends as far west as Santa Monica and as far east as Salt Lake City.

They find her vulgar and distasteful. She's a walking accusation that they're destined to be what she is.

They begin to leave her as soon as they can. They get the hell out after high school. Her daughter gets a scholarship to study in Texas. She comes back every couple of months. Her son does her one better and ends up in Washington, D.C. and only comes back for Christmas and never calls. He's in his own world now. In a world full of polyglots whose parents paid for gap years and cooked them paella and took them on family trips to Morocco. He's not going back.

His sister comes back after college, back to teach elementary school and get married and have a child and be a good person. She's the daughter; she comes back and does her duty, and then takes their mother with her when she and her family move to California. He moves to LA and is almost as distant as he was in D.C. He sees his mother 12 times in 10 years even though he lives 70 miles away. He never invites her out. She comes to visit twice and stays in a hotel both times though he has a spare room. He knows she can't afford it but never asks her to cancel the reservations. They don't talk. It's too hard to go from rooms full of people with graduate degrees, people who've done Fulbrights in Jordan and Vietnam, to a room with a woman who didn't finish high school and whose only experience abroad was a day trip to Tijuana. He wants to forget her. He likes his poor people foreign and distant and abstract. He likes "advocating" for specific groups of them.

She asks for nothing. Leaves him messages that are unrelentingly sunny and pleasant. Still sends him $100 on his birthday, the perfect bills ironed out and pressed into greeting cards that read "For My Wonderful Son" or "For The World's Best Son." She forgives him everything, gives him the benefit of the doubt over and over again. She is proud of him. She displays his degrees and awards on the wall.

He doesn't hear the diagnosis from her. He hears it from his sister. "I didn't want to disturb you, my love," she explains to him. He can see her benignly smiling through the phone receiver. He can see her benignly smiling in a coffin.

He thought of her, his dying mother, in this place. He thought of her sitting quietly in the corner, careful not to embarrass him. She would never feel at home in this crowd. She would try to make conversation with the caterers and the bathroom attendants. She'd call them "Honey." But there was no point thinking about it. She would never go to an academic conference. She would never go to Europe. Death would come for her in a little suburban house in Temecula.

He sunk down just thinking about it. "The gravity of the situation." Literal. It pulled. It made him feel like he was melting into the linoleum floor.

He texted his sister back, slowly. His fingers were stiff. "I'll come out. Promise."

She answered back, instantly. "OK Will. Love you."

And, just like that, he was out of character. Dr. Will Medina, Associate Professor of International Relations at the University of Southern California, here at the International Association for the Study of Forced Migration Conference, surrounded by international lawyers and PhDs and people who worked for the United Nations.

An act. Playtime.

He felt reduced. He wasn't one of them. He was still the son of the housekeeper with the dollar store makeup. He was still ashamed of her. She was dying, and he was still ashamed of her. That she was his mother made him hers. Made him someone who wasn't worthy to be here. One of these things is not like the others.

But then he looked at his phone and saw that he had five minutes until the start of the next panel, and as he had done so often throughout his life, he put his mother and his sister out of his mind. Deleted their messages so he wouldn't be tempted to reread and remember them. Put them away so that he could proceed with something that really mattered to him.

SINK

Rialto

He liked scaring me and he was good at it.

He did it often. Leaning forward in class, he whispered in my ear. Passed me notes. Caught me in the bathroom between periods, took the stall next to mine, and spoke through the door. Taunt-flirting. Each interaction mixing menace and something else I didn't know how to deal with and didn't want to name.

"I've been thinking about you. About what I'd like to do to you."

My grandfather taught me that a man is the sum of his fists. He should be able to prove it by using only his fists, but he can also put instruments in the fists and prove it that way, too. Phones. Hangers. Glasses. Knives. My parents taught me that men sometimes like to mingle fists and instruments and lips. Nothing that I've learned about men over the last decade has disabused me of that.

He'd been in the class for about a month when he first showed me his arms by pushing up his black sleeves so that I could see the scars. Not just lines, but also constellations, letters, numbers. Later, he tugged down his collar to show me the pentagram he carved into his shoulder. He traced its white outline with his finger. With my eyes, I traced his lips and his collarbone and the scar and his scratched hands. I imagined those hands at work scarring and mutilating his skin. I assumed that if they were capable of doing that to him, they were capable of doing that to others.

We talked a lot those months. In classes, in breaks between, in deserted hallways. He needed an audience. I was eager to listen and watch. He was happy to disclose. I was happy to give nothing and take his words and his looks.

Much of it was bullshit designed to shock me. I was a dutiful, closeted, deeply Catholic boy who spent most of my time at school trying to out-achieve my peers and trying to walk from class to class without moving my hips too much. I was easy to shock. I was good at perceiving what other people wanted and pretending to be that thing.

He told me a lot of things. He told me he was a Satanist and that being a Satanist entailed mastering complicated rituals that he enacted in the park near where we both lived. He told me it involved animal sacrifices and that he liked experimenting with them, liked seeing how they reacted to a knife or a lighter before he dispatched them. He usually smiled when he told me these things. I didn't smile, but I wasn't exactly put off. He had pictures of his dog on his social media. It was a Pomeranian. Legit, animal-slaughtering Satanists don't take pictures cuddling with their Pomeranians.

I can picture these things fifteen years later. They are vivid. They are vivid because my eyes soaked themselves in him for hours. Because I sat with the images behind closed eyelids for hours after school. Because I could smell the cream that he used in his long, reddish-blonde hair and because I found that same cream a couple of years later at a drug store and used it in my hair for nearly a decade.

He started bringing razors to class a couple of months in. Showed them to me. Said they were what he used on himself. I shuddered. He saw when I shuddered. He ran the sharp edge of the razor over the skin on the inside of my elbow. The razor grazed it, drew a drop of blood. He looked in my eyes and smiled. I ran into the bathroom and put my arm under the faucet and let the water scald the spot pink and clean.

He showed me a bound notebook that he filled with words he'd written in his own blood. The blood-words were fat and brown and fading. They looked like they were made of tree shit or squashed bugs. I ran my fingers over the ugly, distorted letters and looked at the fine blue veins in his soft hands and was puzzled at the contrast.

He had reddish blonde hair and wide green eyes and pink lips and perfect skin. I assumed his blood would dry vivid red. I assumed anything written in it would gleam slightly.

I had him over to my parents' house just once. It was around April, about a month before his foster parents sent him off to the center in Indio. My mother was out shopping. My stepfather was out of town on a business trip. He lived a few blocks away and rode his bike over.

We sat in my room talking for a while. He wore black shorts. I could see scars on the back of his calves. I could see the pink on the back of his ankle worn into his skin by his Converse sneakers. His sleeves were rolled up. I examined the shiny scars and the fine blonde hairs on his arms. He sat on the bed with his bare legs against the side of my comforter. He laid back on my pillow and let his hair fall over the pillowcase. He touched the inside of my elbow with the tips of his fingers. I let him touch it. I looked at his fingers and his face and told him that he should probably go.

After he was gone, I washed thoroughly the spot that he cut/touched. I pulled my shirtsleeve over it. To this day, when I see a needle or a razor or a knife or a pretty Goth guy dressed in black, I have an urge to clean it and cover it up.

DRIVE

Corona

From the moment they installed it, I was fascinated by the
port-a-cath. Whether bare and exposed or concealed under
a shirt, I would be conscious of it, would look for its outline.
When the needles came out and it fed, when it was stabbed
and fluid flowed into it. When the nurse dabbed it with cotton
and wrapped it up like leftovers. When it lay untouched,
swollen, and red like a cherry. When I imagined it growing,
eating the flesh around it. First, it became a part of them, a
limb, an attribute—Catherine's wheel, Sebastian's arrow, Ray's
port-a-cath. Then, it became a second self. A being under
the skin, pushing the puckered, wrinkled skin up like a tent,
like a pregnant belly. Through the transparent bandage, its
mouth gaped.
　　Years before, when I'd look at them, really look at them—
when the light would catch their face or their wrist would
pulse in my hand or the contours of their back would
be visible through their shirt—I'd see them as flesh and
soul and both mingled and the beauty of one dependent
on and complementary to the other. Every part seemed
meant for the sun. They would always breathe and bleed,
run and regenerate, break and mend. And they would do
it uncorrupted.
　　And then my ideal met the blunt force of reality. Something
else grew in its place—tortured, gaunt, alien. An El Greco
Christ, all knuckles and joints and ribs and angles, all IVs
and catheters and instruments. A distended, sharp body with
strange metallic smells and discolorations. Strange swellings
and lesions and bruises incurred by nothing and sweats
caused by nothing and tortures inflicted by invisible knives
held by no one. A body penetrated and penetrating, sharp to

hold, even the palms of their hands growing dry and hard, as though the skin were being tanned, embalmed on them. It was impossible to touch them without seeing it as an act of sacrifice. Each kiss or embrace administered acted on them to ease their discomfort, even as it increased mine.

Considering who we were, our history, I was surprised to find how much of my love depended on the physical, how much of it was wrapped up in the expectation of familiarity, of constancy.

Now, observing them in the fluorescent hospital light that seemed to follow us everywhere, I struggled to identify the person I had loved in the stranger in the hospital bed. As things fell away, as the person winnowed down, I could conceal reticence, even revulsion behind gentleness. I could excuse the impulse to move away when their hand moved toward mine behind a concern not to break them. When, on those few good days, they'd move their hand down across my stomach or climb on top of me or cover my mouth with theirs, the hard bulge in the chest pressing against me or the stale dryness of the mouth like a sponge left out in the sun, I could convincingly say "I don't want to hurt you" and be believed.

They either didn't recognize it or else they did and made like it didn't matter, like the logistics, the fussing, the arranging, the "Are you really comfortable?" and "Can we get a nurse in here?" was enough. I was afforded the privilege of suffering even by them, the privilege to "process this in whatever way you feel is right for you," whether drunk or angry, binging, crying, staring into space. I had the license to err, to disappear, to seek consolation wherever I thought I'd get it. They bore the long absences in the afternoon, gym trips that took hours, compulsive shopping, excessive drinking. Friends who'd read all the manuals on how to be a good friend to those dealing with terminal illness mimed empathy in my direction, poured out wine, and popped open new bottles when I emptied them, listened when I unloaded endless complaints. Within the vaguely drawn boundaries of reason, it was all acceptable.

But, in hours that they slept, in the lazy late afternoon, in the night silence, in the mornings examining their face, noting every new sign of decline, my thoughts skipped these bounds. I dreamt of passing beyond. I dreamt of release, fingers scraped clean of hospital disinfectant, hours emptied of appointments and consultations, a life in which I wouldn't know the names of a thousand medications. I dreamed of no arrangements and different mouths that I'd never tasted that would never taste of decay. I dreamt of no conceits, of easy guiltlessness, and stakeless, superficial sufferings that I could joke about over drinks. I dreamt of people as garments: bespoke, off-the-rack, throwaway. I dreamt of soaping off the scent of them, regretting them and yet knowing that the regret was insubstantial because they meant nothing. I dreamt of myself resumed, alone.

The thought recurred over and over again. On those endless examination days, waiting for them to return from the linoleum maze beyond the waiting room doors. In the dozens of hours that they lay dazed in a mist of painkillers. Alone at work, imagining what it would be like to leave the office and not have an end time or an end point, not knowing what the hours and days ahead would hold.

At the end of June, the year's steady, continuous decline made way for total collapse. The swelling started in the calves, which grew taught and thick and shiny and blue like a fish, pitted in some places with deep oval recesses the size of a thumb. Then to the feet and the thighs and the arms, until their clothes were impossible to put on and I wrapped them up in blankets. Pain shot through every taut surface until they howled and wept, even with the pain medication. We spent four days in the hospital, waiting, hoping that it would pass with diuretics, ending with the doctor informing us that now would be a good time to look at care options. Their eyes met mine for a moment before I mouthed my refusal, before the doctor followed up with a discussion of the "choices" that now lay before us: voluntarily stopping eating and drinking, palliative sedation, medical aid in dying. An information packet was presented along with a blunt explanation of what death by secobarbital entailed. The peaceful fall into sleep, the peaceful, seamless descent from sleep into death. My head turned from the doctor to the back of their head as they examined the wall, hands shielding their face as they sobbed.

We came home without the packet but with a hospice nurse signed up to attend to their needs while I was at work. After years smiling through needles and examinations, seemingly immune to despair, attitudes changed. They wanted the windows closed, take-out every night, no calls accepted. They refused suggestions to have family or friends over. They berated the nurses, demanded more pain medication, double doses, sometimes getting out of bed to go get them themselves until their legs grew even more irritated. When I was around, they grew angry with me, saying that I was selfish and ready to be rid of them. Confronted with the truth, I would deny everything and act insulted, asserting my position as a partner in all of this and that I was going through this with them. And, then, when the apologies came, as they always did, when that innate kindness and generosity came, I would feel like the imposter that I was, stealing a position of honor that should've belonged to someone else.

I should've come back at the end, drawn by the gravity of death into a final appreciation for all those qualities that I'd seen and taken for granted and, at one point, loved. As they faded, as those qualities spun off them, I should've clung to the remnants.

Even the worst—batterers, serial cheaters, would-be wife-murderers—came back toward the end, with one eye on the clock, yes, but with the other one fixed on that buried, dim something that had been there in the past, the unifying, attracting something that had animated the decision to say that this person, alone, singular, optimistically forever, would do.

The camera obscura that should've focused on them focused on a thousand other things, though. On bills chiefly, piled up in stacks that I had to read and re-read before the amounts materialized, which I lost and searched all over for and eventually found and forgot to pay until collectors called and penalties were piled on and the credit cards came out and I forgot which ones weren't already maxed out. On the thicket of payment plans that automatically ate through our accounts each month, the amounts and durations of which I had lost track of years before. On the coordination of transport and nurses and picking up prescriptions and calling the insurance to make sure the proper percentages of the burden were carried by them per the exact wording of a policy that I had memorized. On my two-hours' drive each day down roads that seemed to teem with people living happier and better lives. On my job, when I could muster the attention needed to send an email or attend to a meeting or provide some half-baked, half-thought-out insight on work that I had muddled through at half the expected speed.

The pink slip came, expectedly, well past time, on a Friday afternoon, with a summons to see a supervisor that I hadn't seen in months. My portfolio was reviewed, my unmet benchmarks recited, and the decision to terminate me dispassionately explained with the cushion of being able to retain our health coverage for six months and three months' salary as severance. The privilege of being labeled "laid-off" extended to the soon-to-be widow. "We truly are sad to see you go," he said and perhaps meant. Time ago, I'd been fairly good at the foreclosure and property holdings business. Handled a good part of the Southwest portfolio, from the Central Coast to East Texas, researching and managing files for thousands of our properties, recommending transfers and sales to other banks and companies. For a couple of years, I even represented the bank at holdings auctions, providing our information on the properties on the block, and in small claims, defending against people who blamed us for their property values plummeting or their houses damaged in an adjoining property's seizure or their belongings lost or damaged during liquidation. Racked up enough frequent flier miles to pay for several vacations, enough office cred to expect a kind of deference. I'd rode that through the past year, where less respected slackers would've been terminated in the first week.

The sun was nearly down when I returned home, the nurses gone, the coffee table spread with paper towels and empty plastic water bottles. They were sleeping on the couch with the television on, their face and chest exposed, pale except for the bright, oil-slicked red crescent around the chin and neck, where a fungal rash had flared up. As usual, asleep or awake, they shivered though the house was baking hot. These deep opiate sleeps lasted through more than half the day usually, through my arrivals home and the upstairs errands of my nights. The strongest sleep possible with the exception of the impending one. Shaken awake, eyes would strain through the eyelids and the shivering setting would be turned up and a rasped "What?!" would squeeze out before the burrowed down person, pulled up from safety for a moment, fell back into unconsciousness.

The last conversation we'd had was five or six days before about a cleaning service. They'd pushed for it, saying that we had to find a way, that the house was filthy and that they were forced to observe it each day without the ability to do anything about it. The house was truly a sty—cups piled up in bedrooms; papers strewn all over tables and desks, shoved into drawers; clothes flung into thick heaps, some half-wet and stinking of mildew. I tried to muster the will to take care of it several times. I'd throw out a garbage bag or two, dump everything into the washer, and then sweep the most offensive messes into the guest bedrooms, the two of them upstairs, where no one would see them. A day or two later, the house would look just as bad.

I wandered upstairs and into my bedroom, piled up with trash bags and dirty clothes. Shut in for the day, the smell of last night's dinner—microwaved breaded fish and some frozen broccoli—hung thick in the air. In the corner, I saw an old duffel bag.

I didn't think about it much. Grab and stuff and go. It's not complicated. Doesn't matter what. Doesn't really matter for what purpose, to what end. Where you will it, the body goes. Off the edge of a building, onto a lit stove, under another person's body, through a summer rainstorm, to Zacatecas or Zimbabwe. And away always sounds, feels better. So, grab and stuff. Wet, dirty cardigan. Underwear. Grab and stuff. T-shirts. Toothbrush. A bar of unused Dove soap in a box. A fistful of prescriptions. Passport. Gun in holster. Four bullets. Grab and stuff and zip. Five minutes and I was on the road, heading east, which, considering the dead end of the Pacific to the west, was not a hard choice. Once on the 10, it was a straight shot through the country, all the way through to Florida and the Atlantic Coast.

I didn't stop until I crossed into Arizona. In the darkness, the windows open, the hot night air whipping into my face. The desert stretched. I disappeared into it.

Around dawn, a few miles away from the Texas border, the first call came. I ignored it. And then, a few minutes later, again, and then again, and then again. Impulsively, I chucked my phone out of the window.

Alongside El Paso, the wall rose up to welcome me, 20 feet of spray-painted cinderblocks topped with a tribal headdress of long, steel nails and the anemic green vein of the Rio Grande down beneath in a steep 30-foot-deep concrete channel crisscrossed with barbed wire. For another hour, I followed it through the ICE checkpoint until disappearing into the interior toward San Antonio. Around sunset, passing the Six Flags on the outside of town with my eyes closing of their own volition, I spotted a Days Inn and, after withdrawing half of our remaining balance of $760, checked in for the night. Fifty-five dollars bought me a second floor "suite" overlooking the empty parking lot, three vending machine vanilla cookies for dinner, and a faucet that sprayed out lukewarm water for a cup of tea. I slept for fourteen hours, waking to a broken air conditioner and a hundred degrees of wet, stinking carpet and a knot in the small of my back where the previous day's drive had carved its initials. The temperature gauge outside read 117 degrees. After turning the car on for ten minutes, air conditioning blaring, observing it from the shade, I got in and pulled out, gripping the still-scalding steering wheel with triple-folded toilet paper. Swaying back and forth between New Orleans and New York, I resolved to go back west six hours to Marfa, where I'd spent a week-and-a-half years before, one of my last vacations before we'd met.

I sped through the wide, enveloping, hot nothingness of West Texas, through towns that had been emptied two or three years before during the deportations. They'd given $300 to each person who reported someone, available in the form of a tax rebate, the PTC. Patriot Tax Credit. You could itemize it in a field on your TurboTax, like a business expense or a mortgage. In California, where it had been countermanded by the state government, outweighed by an equal tax penalty for all who participated, it had limited effect, though in many places, there were those who participated regardless. But here in Arizona and Oklahoma and Kansas and Louisiana and Alabama, where every federal dollar had been supplemented by a state one, cities and towns lost ten or twenty or thirty percent of their populations. Fields went fallow and scorched by the famine sun. Stores shuttered with full sales racks. The remaining people fled to Dallas and Houston and Phoenix and Los Angeles to join an increasingly desperate search for whatever remained of low-skilled jobs, plugging the holes in the customer service machine that computers couldn't yet fill. The rest went into the centers, either as residents or care workers. The homes left behind had been a good part of my portfolio, whole developments full of them in some cases, some abandoned, some seized, all largely worthless, sold in tranches to liquidation companies that picked them clean. For a summer, it'd been the boom business— liquidation and reclamation—as the country set upon its poorest towns and cities, tearing out the contents of ten thousand cul-de-sacs, not only the roof tiles and wood shingles and copper pipes and granite countertops, but also brass beds and leather couches and motorized wheelchairs and playsets and bathrobes and jewelry boxes. The loot was auctioned off wholesale, one giant, national estate sale of the belongings of the civically dead. The remnants still stood, wood frames scraped clean of everything, gutted of their insides, waiting to return into the landscape as nature slowly ate away at them.

What was left was a time capsule stuck in the previous century, a rambling, yellowing, blackened landscape of ruined fast food joints and torn American flags and abandoned Buicks and boarded up car dealerships. Behind the facades lingered the oldest and the frailest and the most hopeless. Every now and then, a gas station would appear, fortress-like, behind a high cinder block wall, with a gate and a bright sign that read "WE'RE OPEN," and you'd have to squint to discern whether or not the sign was new enough to justify a stop or whether it was just another artifact. Over a thousand miles of asphalt, one could lose time as easily as one could lose two million people.

Behind its walls, Marfa was a shocking contrast. In the decade since I'd last been, the luxury hotels and galleries had multiplied, the town now ringed with a skirt of semi-permanent, brightly colored yurts in orange and teal and Aztec prints, ready for 30-something holiday-makers from Austin and Los Angeles and Denver. They flew in on regular Uber flights, ready to spend the weekends downing hibiscus margaritas and watching art house films.

I'd not planned ahead, and with no phone and $220 to my name, there were few options. A gas station attendant directed me thirty minutes out to Alpine, where the Hampton Inn was just at my price point. The money, if I could stretch it, if I could relegate myself to fries and tap water, should last just long enough for the severance money to go through, at which point, I'd decide how long and how far and to what end I would go with this. An hour later, down a road that gradually bled itself dry of affluence, the glam tents and the faux-vintage bars and the tanned young bodies fading into a landscape of blowing plastic shopping bags and weatherworn trailers, I arrived. The muddled green of Alpine was mid-way between the extremes, though the hotel was decidedly grungy and largely vacant, again with an empty parking lot as the focal point. The only signs of activity were a storage lot next door and the liquor store down the street, though a few gray heads were visible in the barbeque joint across the street.

For five days, I stayed inside, drifting between sleep and half-sleep, liquefying as the wall unit strained against the July heat, and venturing out only to buy bags of chips and gigantic glass bottles of cheap beer. On the screen of the old Panasonic box TV, I flipped between grainy tennis matches and Match Game reruns, dancing with the antennae in a doomed attempt to improve the reception. At night, soaked with sweat, unable to sleep, I sat out on the balcony that overlooked the self-storage, puffing on an e-cigarette (an indulgence) and watching the security guards as they made their rounds looking for trouble. Occasionally, my eyes would drift into the hills looking for a light or a shadow, some indication of a hiker or a coyote or a wandering, dehydrated Marfan, swaddled up in a neon green tunic and still lost in a psilocybin parallel universe.

The fifth night, dressed in my damp best, I walked down to the gas station to restock and have a stab at the ATM. The magical $8k appeared on the screen. I attempted to withdraw half of it and met with the word "CARD DECLINED" in fluorescent Tron caps. I made a second attempt with the same result. I scratched at my wallet and the remaining $95. Enough to last another two days, starving. Enough for another two days of whatever this was.

Just as quickly as you strive for independence, just as quickly as you break the place in the world you made for yourself, you remember yourself and resume.

Over the thousand miles back, I resumed my usual posture and mood, my mind readmitting the picture of the house, its red tile and its oak cabinets and the succulents in the front yard, shopping lists and pharmacy drive-thru pick-ups, the sorting of the bills in the breakfast nook. I rehearsed the scenarios that would greet me, the tone and tenor that I would take, the variations on an explanation that I would give. I would blame it on the layoff, on a nervous breakdown, on fear, on being confronted with failure. I would say that I had broken under the pressure, that I had contemplated suicide. I would stop on the way home to get liquored up, ensuring it was evident. I would look terrible when I appeared, filthy and disheveled and sleep-deprived. In my current state, it wouldn't be difficult. I would cry. They would soften before it, as they had so often done before.

By the time I pulled into the driveway the following afternoon, I had resolved on this approach and settled into a persona that would accomplish it. In the mirror, a lined, sweaty, smudged, discolored face stared back at me with the unfocused, heavy-lidded eyes of a drunk. A convincing enough mask.

I opened the door to a cluster of moving boxes and huge black plastic trash bags, fat with clothes. The mess I left had been picked clean, straightened, dishes washed and put away, clumps of wet clothes on the floor removed. The nurses were absent. The television was silent. A piece of paper lay flat on the kitchen counter, with the words "Meridian. – Anita" written on it in red ink.

Three hours later, sitting across from me in a dining room that I'd only been in once over the course of nine years of marriage, my mother-in-law explained to me how it had happened. After a day went by, they called the police and then Anita. Crying uncontrollably, they worried aloud that I was kidnapped or beaten or dead. After five years of no communication, having never been inside the house, she went over and found them lying on the ground in the middle of "a mess unlike I'd ever seen." She dialed 911. The ambulance came and took them to the hospital where they were examined and tested, and it was determined that the cancer had spread to their brain. They regained consciousness and called. Over and over again, a dozen times. On the third day, the pain worsened, and the swelling increased in their legs, stomach, arms. Yellow fluid leaked from their calves, thighs, legs. The pain grew so bad that they passed out, even with the painkillers. The doctors recommended transfer to a care facility and mentioned that it was time to consider "final options." Despite Anita's lack of legal competence to do so, she acceded to both.

On the fourth day, they were taken to Meridian, to the hospice. They regained consciousness again. They called again, hourly, for two days. They spoke to the police and were told that activity had been detected on my card. They called the bank to freeze the card. On the sixth day, with flashes of light appearing in their line of vision and the swelling having gotten so bad that they couldn't move their legs, they requested the Medical Aid in Dying paperwork. They signed it. They called again. In the evening, around 10 p.m., they took 40 milligrams of secobarbital. It took 15 minutes for it to take effect. Anita held their hand, rubbed their head, whispered in their ear. "Rachel, Rachel, my baby. Go to sleep." They'd fallen asleep. Their breathing grew shallower. The attendant called it at 10:36 p.m.

When a body is embalmed, when they strip it and wash it and disinfect it and begin to carve into it, before they paint it up, before they contour and enamel and buff and dress it, they take out most everything that did not come original. They smooth the surfaces. They drain the bloats. They unfill the cavities and remove the more extraneous organs. They syphon the blood from the veins. They remove the IVs and catheters from beneath the skin. A day after the funeral, having requested it from the mortuary, it arrived in the mail. Clean, sanitized blue plastic, with no sign that it had ever touched human flesh.

On nights when the television voices weren't real enough, I'd pull it out of the side-table and run my hands over it, as if expecting that it might, for once, heal something.

ARRANGEMENTS

Jurupa Valley

In February, for the first time in 25 years, it snowed. I woke up before the sun, turned on the morning shows—I like the drone of the traffic reports, although I don't need to listen to them anymore- switched on the coffee maker and saw it through the window. Thought for a moment it might be some fault of the contact lens, dust or something that the solution hadn't washed off.

From the kitchen window, I looked out on the rusty, old mammoth statue flecked with powder staring out from the Discovery Center as though it were about to descend the Alps. If the Alps had chaparral and jutted out behind an empty eight lane freeway.

The last snow came when I was in high school, a light dusting in the winter before I graduated. It fell early on New Year's. Box Springs Mountain and Mount Rubidoux gleamed white in the sunlight for a couple of hours, and the boys next door got out boogie boards and snow hats and mittens and slid all over the grass, both ours and theirs, until the thermometer broke into the high 40s around noon. For a couple of hours, they had a Norman Rockwell January on the lawn. Even the older ones, with ratty mustaches and plugs in their ears and bad attitudes and casual talk of "pussy," whom I knew only too well from various awkward and unpleasant interactions in school. Even they acted like children.

As always, I watched.

"Why don't you go out there?" my father asked me. He and my mother were still married at that point; he was still playing concerned father.

"I prefer to observe," I told him. I still did.

The phone rang. Her. For the tenth time in a week, ready for another round of "Let's get this sorted out." From the other room, a faint but audible moan rose in protest before dying out when the ringer went silent.

The items to sort out: The cremation. The urn. The service. The person to give the service. Back rent. A couch with three large blood stains and cigarette burns on the cushions. A closet full of size 36 jeans and size XL work shirts. The washer and dryer. Hundreds of pictures in two dozen albums, marked from 1967-2022.

And, of course, her. Ex-Mrs. Bray number 2, whose power of attorney made her the functional merry widow. She found him, slumped over in the tub, flecks of blood splattered on the bathroom floor and smeared onto the shower tiles, his body bruised all over. From vodka crawls and dives on the pavement and gropes toward the living room after a half-quart of scotch. From last month's DUI joyride on the 10 that left him liable for damage to a cinderblock wall.

"Hello, honey." The actress. "How you two holding up with the snow?"

She was now, as in the previous 25 years, master of the fate of "the estate." I had no idea whether it contained anything more than the junk I'd seen with my own eyes the day before.

We set a time to meet. One p.m. at the funeral parlor where arrangements would be made at her direction. "I let the family know and I've got everything sorted," she said.

This was the process, then. Between "the woman" (as our grandmother had known her) and "the only son." And two aunts, two sisters, two lawyers, and the estate sale lady. Most of the concerned parties had already expressed their concerns. Aunt #1 wanted the washer and dryer and a lawsuit against "the bitch" for not taking care of him properly. Sister #2 wanted the truck. The lawyer wanted his retainer. The estate sale lady wanted 7% of all proceeds.

I looked out the window, briefly considered putting on
a pair of gloves, then lit a cigarette. On to my third pack of
the week, after six years without, now that ties and vows
and norms of all sorts were obviously on the outs. It's always
best to sense-make with cigarettes. Just as it's always best to
deal with family with them. Cigarettes make good ellipses,
drawing out the time before you must respond. A necessary
pause in which you can formulate what type of self to put on.
Angry or bitchy or fierce or blithe or earnestly sweet. Shall we
be lawyered up or Bible-toting or lettered or crass today? A
few seconds to put on the correct mask.

The cigarette box was half empty by the time I pulled
out an hour later. I took the cigarettes; I left Jeff with the
nurse. He'd had a bad night again for no reason. Or, at least,
on account of no specific stimulus. One of those up out of
bed for hours nights, banging on about something in the
other room, either lost in another world or seeing this one
with a particular terror that it no longer held for me. I slept
through most of it; I dozed off with him locked in the other
room and only awoke around 4 a.m. to the sound of banging
as his head met the already concave drywall. He'd grown
more violent with himself these last couple of months, more
detached from the flesh that housed him. There followed the
usual cajoling, the ranting and tantrum kicks, the moment of
sudden recognition, the smiling and nodding and "It's alright,
honey." And then it was two pills and a glass of water and off
to bed again.

The medication and the nurse would take care of things
now. The blessing of a half-day of medically induced sleep,
reinforced by whatever else was necessary to keep it going.
She had my authorization for it these days, whatever it took,
no matter how strong, to get us through to next Tuesday.
She'd stopped telling me the names of the medications.

The snow had turned to hail had turned to rain had
turned to a heavy gray mist. Clumps of frost still lay on the

hills. I took my usual route through Ontario, past miles of logistics centers and fast food drive-throughs and the airport. Time enough to breeze through the remains of the pack of cigarettes.

The colleges were, as always, oblivious to their context, busy impersonating Bard and Bowdoin and Smith. Today, they were managing pretty well, with the leaves on the trees glimmering with frost and mist on the lawns.

Mike's office was in one of the uglier buildings, a nondescript beige and brick structure at least 50 years old, with brown linoleum on the hallway floors and musty spackled carpeting in the offices. It was visible from the street, at the edge of one of those long rolling lawns where kids stretched themselves out on warm days and inhaled the world. On occasion I saw him there, similarly situated, the long legs stretched out. Once, the husband was there, too, one's head in the other's lap. From a distance, I couldn't make out which head or which lap.

For about a year and a half, I'd made this a weekly habit. "Passing by," I told myself. The nurse would arrive, take over the 24/7 Jeff watch, and I'd get in the car and drive out here. I'd stay for ten minutes sometimes. Sometimes, for an hour. I researched class schedules and lecture times and locations. I determined favorite lunch spots and potential parking locations. And then, I parked on the street and stayed for half an hour, hoping for a glimpse of him.

Only five or six times did I actually see him. Leaving a lecture hall, lying out on the grass. More times than I can count, though, what I thought was him would turn out to be someone else, and then a feeling of being cheated would come, of missing out.

What was the point? The point in examining him, following him? What was the point looking for him here or on my phone screen in the bathroom? Or imagining him in place of Jeff during sex (back when that was a thing)? Or imagining me in place of the husband on one of the idyllic vacations he photographed and advertised online?

I knew his looks. All his looks. I traced and retraced and scrutinized him like grocery store fruit. The full brown of the eyes, with their impossible black lashes. The gray strands at the front of the black cropped hair. The long, pale oval of his face, the high forehead, the thin-boned nose, the m of the full lips. A boy face, incomplete and too precious and deviant. Scheming in the eyebrows, unbalanced in the weak chin, fully aware (and very pleased with the fact) of being watched.

I parked in the usual spot. The fog was thick, but I could see the general outline of buildings and people through it. Most of this side of campus seemed to be empty, far from residence halls and major student gathering places. Absent a couple of wool-swaddled gray figures, it was a lonely scene.

Jeff and I came here once for a day trip—a half day trip— when I was still considering a PhD that came to twelve units of political science for the price of a compact car. We wandered the grounds, two anachronisms with the furrows and crow's feet of our late 30s. He was, as always, in black leather, a latter-day punk, all zippers and asymmetry and out of context snarl. I took him around Claremont Village for an hour, feeling the need to prove that culture was possible here. He was unimpressed, and so we gave up and took the Metrolink back to Union Station, to his territory, to our concrete floors and single paned windows overlooking Pershing Square.

Did he still remember the bars, the boutiques, the restaurants, the shopping trips, and the backyard dinner parties? The friends who worked in dance and design and writing and consulting who disappeared the moment after the symptoms became evident? Our lives there were someone else's now, cast off, alienated from us by illness.

Now an ashtray, the bottom of the coffee cup stared up at me. Third cup of the day, on an empty, knotted stomach that groaned for more.

Blanketed in the fog, anonymous in a wool plaid coat used four times over the course of the decade of its life, I stepped out and examined myself in the car window. Graying, frizzy curls and graying stubble and splotches of raw, bright pink skin underneath. I pulled the coat closed and walked off across the lawn to try to find another cup of coffee.

An hour and a half later, I pulled up the long drive to the mortuary, past Michelangelo reproductions blackened from freeway exhaust. A white columned, faux-neo-classical building housed the sales floor, the flower shop, the refrigeration facilities, and a smaller chapel that they used for the less popular clients. It was familiar territory. They'd done our grandparents' funerals in quick succession twenty years ago, pitiful, open-casket affairs, with half a dozen people other than the family attending and a dial-in priest who came up for ten minutes, gave a standard eulogy, and cashed out. At the vault ("The Mausoleum of Christian Heritage"), both of them were elevatored up on a terrifyingly rickety accordion contraption. The "Memorial Counselor" folded the flag and gave it to my mother and "Taps" came over the speakers. We came every six months after that, into the brown carpeted bottom floor of the facility, the front of which was plastered over with what Forest Lawn called "the largest Christian mosaic in the world," depicting scenes from the life of the Robert Powell Jesus. A button on the front, if pushed, would get a Charlton Heston impersonator to explain it to you.

Our mother's funeral a year ago had managed just a bit more dignity than that; she, at least, had living friends, in-laws, co-workers, cousins. And detailed directives—down to readings, colors, guests—for the exact opposite of what had been done with her parents. It had been a reasonably large funeral, conducted by a priest she had known for years, punctuated by heart-felt and reasonably authentic tributes to her.

By the time I arrived, the Bray women had already been assembled in a large but dark office full of ocean and nature scenes and light classical music. A young woman in a black pantsuit and fake pearls had begun to lead them through a white binder of necessary paperwork. In her usual style, Marion had taken the helm, a position of place in the center, my aunts and sisters several feet away to her left, clustered together as though trying to outweigh her on a scale of importance.

With two exceptions, they stood as I entered, my aunts rushing forward in earnest, intent on depriving her of the role of mistress of ceremonies. The typical exchange followed: hugs and tears and expressions of sorrow and "It has been such, such a long time" and "How's Jeff doing?" and "I hope you know how much he loved you." Strange old ladies, these, wearing grandmother costumes, expecting something— familiarity, regret, affinity—that I probably failed to adequately impersonate. Sixteen years may as well have been fifty. Lauren followed, all emotion, all tears. And then Alex, all business, somber and quiet, easy.

Marion received me with crossed legs, wearing a beige business suit and the bobbed black hair that had always been her signature. "Hello, honey." No hugs, everyone knew better than that. A burgundy leather USC folio lay on the seat next to her, and a manila envelope marked with a label reading "James Bray-Documents" had been unclasped, its contents spread over the dark wood. A worn leather checkbook lay to her right. The mood was "closing the deal." I could deal with closing the deal.

The woman in the black suit walked us through a steady procession of signatures. There was initial uncertainty over the chain of command. "Who's the next of kin? You, Mrs. Bray?" Silence. No takers.

"My father was divorced." My voice. "My sisters and I are next of kin." Adjusting the papers in front of her, Mrs. Bray smiled. The aunts smiled. The suit smiled. The sisters and I smiled.

We signed here and there. The release of the body, the death certificates. Me, then Lauren, then Alex, passing the papers down the assembly line as they were presented. I wondered who would pay for all this. I still had student loans on me at 42, because he refused, despite the '68 Corvette and the '69 Alfa Romeo and the 5,000 square foot house in Pasadena and the matching Hummers and the collection of $1000+ Lladro figurines, to front the cash. And now, by virtue of sharing 50% of the blood on the shower tile, I was expected to put my signature on the page and take responsibility for a man who had so rarely taken responsibility for me. I added another resentment to the running list.

We proceeded through the checklist: programs, music, service, flowers, cremation. Once brought up, each item hovered in the air, no one eager to decide until, by default, Marion chimed in. I assumed this indicated she intended to pay for everything. I was more than happy to let her do so.

We were walked up to the second-floor showroom to select an urn. After some discussion with the aunts, Marion hit on a particularly ugly but surprisingly expensive stone box, carved with a cross and footprints and the words "When you saw there were only one set of footprints, it was then that I carried you." Chicken Soup for the Schmaltzy Soul. Evidently, she was still stuck in those ironic years of before-dinner prayers and AA mantras that stretched out in between mutual affairs. "Of course, I will be paying for this," she said. She smiled. My aunts smiled. My sisters and I smiled.

I wandered off from the group for a second to examine the coffins, all familiar, unchanged through twenty years. They apparently don't require updates; the dead do not complain about lack of variety.

Through my headache, I heard life intrude as they devolved into discussion of wedding arrangements and home renovations and grandchildren—a seventh one for one, a third one for the other. With payment clear, they'd apparently resolved to pretend at closeness, exchanging pictures, stories, niceties.

Amazing, what people are capable of temporarily forgetting.

A frigid rain came with dusk, and mercifully short goodbyes, and everyone dispersed to be themselves in private. On the way back home, the center called. More unsigned paperwork to attend to, release forms, discharge forms, medical report acknowledgement forms, medical liability forms. Would we be retaining Jeff's nursing service? Would he require supplemental care? Would we require assistance for the move on Tuesday? Over the speaker: Yes. Yes. Yes.

The rain stopped, and in its place, as the temperature dropped and the sky blackened, the flecks of white returned. On my phone screen Mike's face popped up with the words "Hey mister. Were you on campus earlier? I saw a silver fox in a trench coat fitting your description."

I turned off into a service station, and in the car, with the snow gathering on the windshield, finished the remains of the pack while I thought through what I should text him in response.

COUCH-DWELLERS

Moreno Valley

Twenty-five years on a couch. Twenty-five years in a cell of their own making. In the afternoons when the light hit the dust and the popcorn ceiling shone and the carpet stank and you could taste the staleness in the air. In the nights, their faces lit by TV reruns and infomercials. In the mornings, when the sunshades strained to keep out the world. Through it all, still there.

"Can you really believe them?" we said to each other. With sneers, we discussed the details. The smells of their bodies. Their unkempt hair and beards, the patches of gray in them. The holes in increasingly worn and dirty pajamas. The noise of their laughs and sighs and tears, crashing pans, running microwaves, drunken fights, videogame battles—their nights. The missing food—blocks of cheese, packets of tortillas, boxes of crackers, bags of burritos—as soon bought, as soon disappeared. The dirty dishes they left on the tables and in the sink. The sudden, guilty rush to cover themselves when they were caught hunched over the computer after midnight and the insultingly unconcealed pile of Kleenex left over in the wastebasket the next morning.

Their worthlessness and our frustration were constants in our lives. At a hundred dinner tables, we complained about how we would never have dared, how our consciences wouldn't have permitted it. We would've been beaten out of it by our parents, members of a generation that knew how to deal with laziness and stupidity.

Inevitably, after a glass of wine or two or three, we would turn to resolution, to plans of action. Ultimatums. Forced job applications. Throwing them out on the street. Reporting them for antisocial behavior. Committing them to care. The next day, the next week, we would turn them around, salvage something resembling men. We would act as parents—with sternness, firmness, and common sense.

But, at the end of the night, we came home to them as they were. To these lazy, dirty, unambitious, unclean, immature, incapable beings we made. Made with care, with precision, with constant discussion and consultation, with expert advice along the way from a hundred supporting players. Made with worry and concern, with rushing and wrinkles and pieces of ourselves.

We deserved them. Hadn't we reared them on our tastes, on our routines, on our preferences? So many put-off family vacations, so many deferred dreams, so many tired take-out evenings. Hadn't we taken charge of their moral and religious education? Twice-a-year church services. Poorly concealed indiscretions. Hadn't we given them their chief models for marriage and family, for responsibility and sacrifice? Long silences punctuated by the verbal assaults of two people who knew each other too well.

And now we lived with the results and did our best to reconcile ourselves with the knowledge that they would be the primary occupation of the final chapter of our lives. That thoughts of their welfare would be on our minds at our ends. That we would bear responsibility for ensuring their welfare until we died.

And then citizen's allowance checks came. The blessing of state support. And it was a blessing, although they were eligible only for 50% benefit. Now, for the first time in twenty-five years, they had their own money and, to our great surprise, a sudden eagerness to use it. Money for Game Centers and vape lounges and even enough to rent a co-work space for part of the day. Time away from us, like a return to school.

They began to spend a few hours a day in the company of people like themselves. To play games, go out for drinks, hang out on weekends. Friends rematerialized, both male and female. Actual lives, actual happenings, though most of them shared similar personal histories and trajectories, long-suffering parent-caretakers whose joy at their children's absence must have mirrored ours.

That first spring and summer, after a decade of nothing, was a dense droplet of hope. The days and nights out. The phone calls and plans. The resurgence of personalities and interests that we had almost forgotten existed. Long buried tastes in dress and food and activity were suddenly uncovered, as though our teenage children had returned from hibernation, though in bodies that no longer looked like theirs. Derek, technical and interested in the mechanics of things, with his schematic mind. Vincent, with his appreciation for the grotesque and the macabre, always rambling and tangential. Both boys returned in all their glorious, beautiful, unwieldy geekiness.

That July, for the first time in at least a decade, we took them out shopping to Victoria Gardens. Made a day of it, throwing money around carelessly, grinning at the spectacle of two men in their mid-40s looking through the sales racks at Urban Outfitters next to 19-year-old college kids. And afterward, haircuts, watching the strands of greasy, graying hair fall. And then dinner at Yard House, discussing plans for the upcoming week, engaging them in something like a conversation for the first time in years.

It is amazing how durable hope is. How, even with thousands of days and nights of experience, the capacity to believe that change can happen remains. How knowing someone—really, knowing them—we can, with the frailest of reasons, believe that all those decades of experience can fall away and something else can emerge through sheer force of will. Even when you remember all those countless, identical times before when hope buckled and broke under the pressure of reality.

We bought it. Totally. We saw the haircuts and the new clothes and the friends and the brushed teeth, and we bought that this was a different world. Each small step was a triumph. Attention to hygiene. A muttered hello to the check-out girl. A big fucking deal.

That fall, our expectations were heightened by the sudden proposition of a weekend trip to Temecula with a mixed group of people their age. They were all forty-somethings on public assistance, worn out to various degrees, unmarried and childless. Their stories were similar: middle class suburban families, college educations, early stints in the workforce, years of aimlessness, lives of sustained adolescence beyond the point at which that can pass as "finding yourself." None seemed objectionable. No drug or alcohol problems were in evidence. No perversions were visible to the naked eye.

They arranged to stay for two nights at Pechanga using one of the group's parents' credit card and high-roller benefits to book a suite that came with free buffet and access to the hotel spa. New clothes were carefully folded into borrowed suitcases. Promises were made to avoid the blackjack tables and be mindful of the potential negative effects of mixing depression medication and too much alcohol.

That Friday afternoon came, and a nondescript, late-model white van. Through the tinted windows, we could make out a party of three men and two women in total, all but the driver (who introduced himself as "your sons' friend, Kyle") diligently looking away from us as we waved goodbye. Suitcases loaded, embarrassing goodbyes avoided, the group rounded the corner and disappeared.

Around noon the next day, we got a call. A woman's voice informed us that our son, Derek, had been admitted to Temecula Valley Hospital that morning, and that he had suffered cardiac arrest en route. She said he had lost consciousness, that hospital staff had done everything they could to resuscitate him, but that, despite their best efforts, he had passed away approximately an hour ago.

The nurse let us know that the hospital staff had removed all tubes and IVs from his body and that they had laid him out in a bed in the ICU for us to view and say our goodbyes, if we could get there in the next hour. "He's ready for you when you come," she said. "And your other son, too."

Breaking down the next hour or so into its constituent movements, we got up from the table, turned off the coffee pot, grabbed our jackets, checked that the doors were locked, turned off the lights, got in the car, turned off the radio, opened the garage door, backed down the driveway, closed the garage door, left the house. We drove down Alessandro and onto to the 215, past March Field and the veteran's cemetery, past Perris, Sun City, Menifee. We passed country clubs and beige stucco and red tile and green lawns and brown, rocky hills and Diamond Valley Lake, where we used to fish with the boys. And then into the hospital lot, grasping for the handicap placard, pulling into the closest space, turning off the engine, exiting the car, and walking toward the sliding doors.

"We're here to see our son's body and to pick up our other son."

The nurse, a rotund, kind-looking little thing in her 50s, showed us through, directing us with a soft whisper that she must have always used in these situations. She led us down a set of halls that gradually shed their color, from the salmon and seafoam of the reception area through a light blue corridor, then onto shale gray, and finally, the pure blankness of the ICU, its linoleum floor gleaming up at us like white teeth.

She was all whispers, gently instructing us to follow her. "This way, please."

We were led into the room. All white, television off, hospital bed at an angle, as if he were still present and about to peel open a pudding cup or turn on the radio or something. The constant hum of machines from other rooms, where patients who still needed them clung on to life.

He was naked, his bare, pale shoulders the same shade as the sheet. His eyes were closed. His eyelashes looked wet, separated, as though someone had applied mascara to them.

His skin was already skin and not skin, already dead, already at a remove from breezes and pools and sand and sweat and car steering wheels and cigarettes and new shirts and other hands. It was already unfamiliar, already something rather than someone. His hair looked shockingly red—boy red, wagon red, fire engine red. So red it seemed to swallow up the strands of gray.

He was forty-seven. Middle aged—not quite correct. End aged. End date. Expiration date. This white block of person. This strange, alien slab. Nothing more for it to do, and nothing more to do with it.

And yet he looked, to both our eyes, younger than he had in a long time. Younger, smaller, cleaner. A white, sanitized, marble model of a son.

Chairs were set out for us. Old, sweat-stained upholstery, faded in the seat with wear, shining where so many bodies had rocked and seized and shuddered. How many slumping, shattered, waning people had observed death happen here? We sat in their impressions. We watched the body. We memorized it. Every wrinkle, every plane, every color, every curve. This marvel of geometry, its softness hardening, convex soon to become concave as the architecture of his body collapsed.

The shadows turned, admitting the sun through the windows. It was the kind of nauseous, hospital light that evokes iron in the mouth and alcohol swabs on forearms. "You can touch him," a voice said. The nurse was still there. Never left, apparently.

Some time passed before a doctor came. "Which of you is the mother?" We were both too tired to respond, to correct her. She intuited the truth from our silence. "Oh... I'm very sorry for your loss. For both of you."

She used the same tone of voice as the nurse, the whisper with notes of concern. Even so, direct. To the point. "It'll be some time before the toxicology report comes in and we won't be sure until an autopsy is performed, but it looks likely that prescription drug abuse played some role in your son's death."

Exit, ghost. Enter, paperwork. Clipboards were presented to us. Clipboards that had papers on them that we signed. We didn't ask what we were authorizing. We didn't care.

We left the body where it was and came back out into the world. Vincent sat in another, identical salmon and seafoam waiting room, legs splayed wide, arms locked against a chair, wrists adhered to the wood by zip-ties. His eyelids fluttered. His shoes lay several feet away from him. He'd evidently kicked them off.

The catatonic moaned, arms rigid for a second as they struggled against the restraints. "I couldn't...." Probably true. Whatever he couldn't do, probably true.

"We'll see that those are removed," the nurse whispered and pointed to the zip-ties. She was still there.

They cut the plastic cuffs off him, gave him another sedative, shoved him into a wheelchair, and handed him off. At this point, there were more clipboards.

We briefly discussed the possibility of calling people. Why not save that for tonight, though? Bathroom breaks were made and faces washed and looked at in mirrors. And then, jackets were zipped and keys fished out of the purse and our one remaining son rolled away and sliding glass doors walked through and car door unlocked and car door opened and car turned on and space pulled out of and gas pedal pushed and rewind all the way back to home.

We buried Derek in the plot that we'd bought for ourselves. A priest who never knew him gave the eulogy from a list of adjectives that we emailed to her in a Word doc saved as "OrderofServiceDerek.docx." She recited the poems and verses that we'd selected. Derek Walcott. Robert Ingersoll. "He wasn't particularly religious," we said. How the hell did we know what he believed? We barely knew anything about him.

About a dozen people came, all of them friends of ours, all of them proficient in the mores of old-age friendships. A family funeral is the price of a child's wedding invitation or a cruise to Mexico. It's what you do.

Vincent did not attend.

He went back on the couch. Well...between the couch and his room and his brother's room, which was now left to fall under his jurisdiction. Four TVs were now at his disposal and the kitchen and the office and the outside garage and the gap between the garage and the retaining wall right outside our bedroom where they both liked to smoke in the late evenings. We could hear him there after dark, pacing, inhaling, murmuring illegibly to himself. Or in the living room, with some television comedy on and muffled laughter. Or in the kitchen past midnight, pouring glasses of booze for himself and microwaving up something to eat.

The citizen's allowance checks continued coming, a lump sum $3,000 death benefit and weekly ones for him. He didn't take notice of them. For a while, they piled up on the furniture, unspent, before we decided to take them as long-overdue rent.

Months elapsed. We took a vacation, alone, for the first time in years. Back to Croatia and Montenegro where we honeymooned fifty years ago. Dubrovnik, bright and Italian and in love with life, with its red roofs and its limestone walls and its smattering of antique Western and Chinese tourists. Kotor, gray and Byzantine, winding up the hill above the bay, with its band of exiled Russian oligarchs. Our gray heads bobbed along with the gray heads of the other winter holiday-makers. Buttoned-up, tweedy sorts of people, spending away their home equity. Youth, such as it was, came in summer, muscled and tanned and sailing into port trading on its privileges.

At a restaurant on the water in Budva, we decided to move. The house was a museum, brown and creaking and dusty and full of bad memories. It was a stage on which we'd played too many familiar scenes, passed too many identical days, made too many unsuccessful choices. Bad turns had happened there. Bad ends had been set in motion. It was in the house's bones. Paint and stucco and wood flooring and new tile and a new roof and new landscaping couldn't remove it. There was no point anymore clinging to the edges of something that no one valued or missed. The stimuli of nostalgia were thirty years past, and now even the inner substance of it had rotted away.

All that was left now was him, the last remnant, the "I couldn't...." Sinking back into his old habits with the addition of an unknown slew of new ones. Back, but doing double-duty now, tottering around the house and into the yard and behind the garage for a smoke and asleep at 11 a.m. and up at 8 p.m. A floating plastic bag of a man, thinking, apparently, that this system we'd established was a set one. He depended on it and, like all dependencies, it sucked him dry. What good would it do him to spend the next twenty years as he had the previous twenty, sleepwalking through days and nights, with an assist from SSRIs and his mommies? Wombmates and tombmates.

Well...enough. No more of that. Resolve. Over mussels and Montenegrin wine. Adults, common sense adults, do resolve.

We returned. He had not burned down the place. He had not done anything to the place, as expected. Garbage heaped up in the kitchen. Dishes in the sink. Clothes unwashed in the hamper and then, presumably, reworn, and then thrown back in the hamper. Cigarette butts stacked up in the ash trays. Mail strewn about.

We caught a glimpse of him a couple of hours later after sunset. A sleepy hello from the good morning man.

Admitting him was a simpler process than either of us expected, and cheaper, too. They were everywhere now, adult care facilities, and for younger and younger people. Separated by age group. Teens at this facility. Twenty-somethings at this one. Thirty-somethings here. Themed, some of them, like summer camps: religious, musical, theatrical, political, gluten-free, Republican, Democrat. Ones for lower and higher orders. Ones for languages and hobbies and skills. Ones for makers, writers, humanitarians, activists, techies. And, the majority, unthemed ones for unthemed people. It was amazing Montessori hadn't gotten into the business. Or Leisure World.

They'd grown more numerous for the young ones than for the old. We, those of our age, had "aging in place" to look forward to, kept in our residences, in our quiet communities by a wide array of technologies designed to prevent us from discomfort, disgrace, death.

For the young, "adult activity communities," "adult life communities," "adult purpose communities" multiplied. Sometimes, adjectives were appended, like "thriving" or "vital" or "youthful." Subsidized by the government, accepting citizen's allowance, designed to house unnecessary suburban human refuse. Most states passed legislation to enable parents to commit their children without their permission and with considerably less difficulty than one might go about committing a manic depressive on a tear. They were necessary, these storage facilities for those whom society had no use.

We met with the real estate agent and with the "Placement Specialist" on the same day. Cursory questions were asked, papers were signed, deadlines were set.

We put the house on the market and decided to look for places on the Central Coast, 60+ and gated. Some place quiet and green and overgrown with vegetation. Someplace small, a bungalow or a condo built for two.

As for Vincent, he would be taken first to a Placement Center, where a battery of tests and interviews would be administered. An algorithm would use his responses to make an optimal placement for him. "We find that better decisions are made through this process than by parents or the member. It tends to work out happier for everybody. As for contact, we find that it's really best to limit communication for at least a year. It makes the transition smoother."

Deferring, as always, to the experts, we decided to follow that advice. In the years to come, we could almost pretend (and we often did) that he—that they—had just gone away to Temecula for the weekend.

KIN

Rancho Cucamonga

Before Marina left, we were distant, polite. Days passed
without talking, without needing to talk. Days passed with
notes left on kitchen counters for me to sign and beds made
when the house was empty after she'd taken Will off to school.
At games and recitals, her eyes crossed me on their way to
their real target.

Will was born three weeks early. I was out of the country
on business and learned by voicemail. I looked at pictures
of him at a trattoria on the Campo dei Fiori. A boy with my
eyes, held by the woman who was his real mother, who spent
years grinding me down for him. I came home five days later
to find an established hierarchy. Marina fed him. Marina
changed him. Marina bought clothes and toys and decorated
the nursery and put together meals and auditioned friends
and arranged swimming lessons and selected the preschool.
Eyes only for each other, they occasionally appeared and
acknowledged my presence only to disappear back into the
private world they built. On occasion, I'd be tasked with
driving him to school. On occasion, I'd watch him and his
friends play when Marina shopped. On occasion, I'd attempt
to connect to him, fail, and then go back to something that
really mattered to me.

The boy grew into my echo: my voice, tics, preferences.
Strangely, none of Marina's. It was rare for us to spend a full
hour together. In the morning, they left before I woke up,
leaving bowls of cereal or cups of orange juice on the table for
me to clear. At night, invariably, they ended up in the same
room together, watching some children's television show or
playing a game or riding through night terrors. And yet, he

inherited my voice, my shyness, my anxiety, my face, and my hair. Nature, triumphing over nurture.

And then it happened.

In the months before, there were the remote stories of others, names on appeals from nonprofits that we sent recurring contributions to, minute-long reports on local news. There were protests in Los Angeles and New York at the news from Arizona and Texas. There were denunciations from the governor, outrage for the cameras. Friends and colleagues spoke theoretically about the impact on people in communities where our only experience had been driving through on the way to someplace else. In company, those few times a year when we left Will with someone else, a mention might come up of politics and Marina would, in her usual way, bat it away quickly and change the subject. TV, gossip, travel, the small, daily troubles involved in child-rearing. Those few minutes a day when we were alone, we didn't talk about anything beyond that, didn't feel the need.

The day it happened, Marina left the house while I was still in bed, dropped Will off at school, and headed to the store. She did whatever she usually did there, inventory or reshuffling the displays or reconciling the previous day's sales. It was her business, her project of the past two years to which she devoted maybe 30 hours a week and to which I devoted $150,000. It was always in the red, always dependent on increasingly large infusions of money from our savings. But it gave her something to do.

She opened. The day's sales were standard—another way to say "bad" but not remarkably so. She sold $180 worth of merchandise. She passed the time, somehow. She took her lunch at 1:00, drove off down the street, and that was it.

Months later, I'd wait until Will went to sleep and leave him in his bed and retrace her movements that day. Drive out to the storefront, which still had the glossy "ITALIAN SUITING: Up to 40% OFF" and "DESIGNER SUITS AT WHOLESALE PRICES" signs in the window. Sit for a while, examining the empty racks, the sales counter strewn with papers. Drive past the shells of the Macy's and JC Penney's and Barnes and Noble, past great, empty, football field-sized surface parking lots, park in front of the restaurant, and imagine her walking in and being walked out.

That day, she went to a place down the street, a Mexican restaurant. She ordered, sat down, waited for the food to come out. A group of cops entered. In my imagination, I see three bull-necked white guys with brawny, tattooed arms. In reality, there were two Latino guys in their mid-30s and an older white female. They were federalized county cops. They frequented places where they knew they would find targets to fill the quotas they'd been assigned. They showed up at *quinceaneras*, community events, weddings, concerts. They patrolled neighborhoods, stalked Facebook groups. They staked out nonprofits and religious organizations. And they regularly made the rounds at restaurants.

The cops casually appeared in front of her and asked for her name and identification. They examined the state driver's license she offered, marked with the words "Federal Limits Apply." They asked for the passport. They watched her stammer out a response, let her stew in silence through a string of heavy, breathless seconds. They asked her to accompany them outside. She did.

Outside the restaurant, they chatted for a few minutes. Essential information, names, addresses. One of the group suggested that they would be better able to resolve "this situation" at the station. She was ushered into the car. Not into the back, but into the passenger's seat. Music was turned on. Small talk was had. The unreassuring reassurance "I'm sure we'll get this sorted out" hung in the air.

They drove her to the neighborhood police station, a place with a bulletin board of local happenings, with a comfortingly shabby brown shale exterior, with a child-painted "Protect and Serve" banner. There, she realized that this meant serious trouble. In the conversations of the next few months, before the silences descended and lengthened, she never quite remembered when the understanding had set in. Whether it had been when they asked for her phone and wallet. Whether it had been when the uniformed officers gave way to a buttoned-up man in a two-piece brown suit. Whether it had been when she noticed the sky reddening with the approach of sunset.

By nightfall, she was booked, pictures and retinal scans and fingerprints taken for the record. Her remaining belongings were confiscated to be returned to her on the other side by the Mexican Federal Police. She was placed in a black sedan marked "ICE" and removed down the 215 freeway. She stayed the night at a detention center in Menifee. After a night, a bus took her to San Diego for final processing and lodging any potential appeals, which were heard within the hour by a clerk. Prompt dismissal came within the same day, and then another bus came and took her through the guard towers and on to Tijuana for processing by the Mexican police. From start to finish, 32 hours.

I was in LA when the news came that she hadn't showed up at school for pick up time. Two hours later, I arrived to find Will sitting out on the curb in front of the school, little boy knees reddened by the September sun. Without words, he climbed into the back-passenger's seat. Without words, we drove to Marina's mother's house.

Together, we made arrangements and improvised lies to tell the boy. We wrapped him in a blanket of cousins and aunts and uncles and food. Only when we stood outside alone did we acknowledge the possibilities that lay before us. A dead body in a gutter, a live body tied to a chair, an unidentified body strapped to a hospital bed.

I lay awake in the empty, quiet house all that night. My house, mine before we met, bought with my money, furnished with the products of my work, but hers, thoroughly hers. Empty bed. Empty boy's room. Empty sink, with no bowls of cereal or cups of milk to wash up. Empty half of the driveway. Sad, like a soundstage without actors. Sad and purposeless.

The following evening, the call came from across the San Ysidro crossing. The operator announced it first in Spanish and then in English. "You are receiving a collect call from a reception center operated by the Mexican Federal Police. If you accept the call, your telephone service provider may charge you additional fees." The Mexican government processed paperwork there, ran checks on citizenship, began deportation proceedings for anyone who wasn't Mexican. A bank of phones awaited those who had been deported; translators for those who didn't speak Spanish; wiring services; temporary accommodation and transport. The most desperate, the most connectionless could stay for a few days in the facility. The rest tried to get back, though the chances of success diminished with each passing year.

Her voice scratched its exhaustion into my ear through the receiver. My name, repeated. My name and the words "I'm sorry." At least half a dozen times. "Em, I'm sorry. Em, I'm sorry...."

I stammered out a "What happened?"

She told me the story.

She had already called her mother to arrange next steps, to ask for help connecting with relatives to the south until she could come up with a plan to get back. It would be some time before she could connect with the type of people whom she could trust. What was most easily available was the classic scam: gouge and ditch or extort and leave half-dead. To find the real thing, honest greed, would take weeks. Maybe months. In the meantime, she said, I would have to take over her portfolio: take care of Will as best I could. She would need money to find accommodation and pay for essentials. I agreed to wire $5,000, which should see her through the month in some place safe and clean and quiet. Once settled, she would check in and speak with Will. It would, hopefully, take no more than a week.

She offered an "I love you," a strange, hollowed out, echoing "I love you" that shook in the plastic bell of the phone receiver. I reciprocated. And then a drawn-out silence with neither of us sure what lay on the other end of a goodbye. Then the line went dead, and it was over.

That afternoon, I went to see Will at his grandmother's. He stayed in his cousins' room, Marina's nieces, whose mother had left the previous year. They were an inhospitable duo. On one or two occasions, they corrected him when he'd called them his cousins, told him that they heard that they weren't actually related. They were told off, in English by Marina and in Spanish by their grandmother, her way of indicating an especially grave sin. Now they treated him with a kind of impatient standoffishness, whispering in corners, leaving rooms as he entered.

In the best of circumstances, he was a fragile boy, emotional, breakable. With Marina, he could be joyful, bubbly, light. But alone, without Marina, he turned sullen, quiet, dark. His natural tendencies were toward the corner, toward disappearing into the background. In that, as in so many things, he took after me.

He was in the girls' room when I arrived, sitting alone on the carpet. Through the window, muffled twin laughter intruded. I sat down next to him. He gave no sign of recognition or acknowledgement. "Will? Will, honey, we need to go home now." Nothing. "Will, we need to go home now and sleep in our own beds and get ready for school tomorrow."

Under the brows, the blonde head still down, two eyes skimmed me before moving down again. "Will, come on. We need to go." And then again, no response. I touched his arm softly, my hand brushing his wrist. He slapped it away. "Come on!" My hand grabbed his wrist and tugged up, and his other hand formed a fist and met it, the head still down. I forced him up. He looked at me for a moment, let out a grunt, and landed a swift, forceful kick on my shin.

On the way home, darkness shrouding his face in the rearview mirror, I remembered a hundred other drives home with Marina in the front seat and him in the back, singing and laughing together, smiling and feeding off each other. I would drive them with my eyes focused on the road, nothing on the brain but getting to bed, getting to work, getting anyplace else but there. Absence of thought, absence of love. The boy knew it, felt it. He knew me as a stranger, the woman who drove and picked up after things and set the table and then disappeared. And I knew him as an extension of Marina, a favor to her.

It was simple enough to go about the mechanics of motherhood. Wake the boy up. Make him breakfast. Make sure he's washed and puts on his clothes and has his backpack. Pile him into the car. Drop him off. See he makes it into the building all right. Later, pick him up. Pile him into the car again. Drive him home. Make him dinner. Send him off to bed. Checklists. Keeping things moving so that they don't stop, so that greater discomforts don't rise up to replace ordinary ones. And a little scowl to thank me for all of it.

While I had thought that he was just ignoring me before, just treating me with a kind of disinterest, I now realized that he actively disliked me. He understood the general flow of our days together, that things would have to be done with his cooperation, and he usually did them, but they were disembodied movements with every attempt made to avoid looking at or talking to me. He'd have preferred that a machine be created that could make him his meals or lay out his clothes, a Jetsons robot-parent with a function to pour milk in his cereal and drive him to school. I learned to treat him that way.

Two weeks passed uncomfortably. I mentally began to keep track of the words he spoke to me each day. A dozen or so. Enough words to populate the spare moments in which I caught glimpses of him before he disappeared into his room and closed the door. Across the hall, behind that door, my seven-year-old teenager, with his distinct territory and life.

Finally, after dinner one night, a phone call came from Marina. Down the line, the voice muffled. Distant family had put her in contact with a guy in Mexico City who was considered experienced in getting folks safely back across the border through connections with people in ICE. He was wary of connecting with new people, took his time fully checking them out, doing research on their backgrounds and the reasons for deportation. He was many times more expensive than some of the other options, but people vouched for his relative reliability and honesty. She would meet with him in two or three months and decide then whether to continue or not.

At the edge of my eyeline, boy pajamas and the two stranger's eyes came into view, observing me. My eyes met his with a nod. He stepped up and took the phone into his hands.

Tears spilled out over the small, red face. And, over and over again, "I miss you, mommy. I miss you, mommy. I miss you, mommy," in the plaintive way that children have, thinking that their words will conjure up a different reality if they say them with enough force. They spoke for thirty minutes, the boy unburdening himself, nodding with recognition, smiling, lifting in the light of convincing reassurances. He turned in my direction, the face deflating again as he remembered which parent was with him and which one was not. A nod came, and then a "Mommy wants to speak with you." Half the words he'd spoken to me that day.

"You need to do a better job of being present for him." Somewhere, at some point in the conversation, there had been an indictment of my conduct, quietly sandwiched in between the tears and the "I love you's." There was no mistaking her anger. "You can't just disappear into your own world. He needs a mother." Yes, but not this one. Not the one he had on hand.

In the days after, my attempts at concern and doting met with the same result. He lived only for the nights, for the ringing of the phone, and for the brief time when I answered before handing things off. The calls came frequently. Every day after dinner. Depending on Marina's access to serviceable internet, we grew accustomed to daily calls that lengthened to hours. By appointment, the boy would wait by the computer in the evenings, waiting to see her face on the screen. They would stay there for an hour or more as I sat off to the side, out of the eyeline of the camera. As goodbyes were exchanged, I would emerge, wrap things up, and bundle him off to bed.

The date of her meeting with her honest people-smuggler approached. She said she would be gone for two days but would check in regularly by text and email. The goodbyes the night before were especially excessive in their emotional intensity, in the number of "I love you's" and "I miss you's."

A string of texts came before and after the flight to Mexico City. She was in transit to the airport, on the plane, safely arrived, on her way to the house where she would be staying with a family friend.

And then, silence. Repeated texts and calls unanswered.

The boy asked for an update. I told him that I had exchanged words with her over email, that she said to tell him "I love you" and that they would chat the next night.

And then came the morning and an equal silence, and a day off work and calls with her mother and her cousins, brainstorming ways to determine what had happened. And the second night, still nothing, and a lie to see us through to the next morning and then sleeplessness, sketching images of the ugliness that the next few days had in store. And through all of it, Will still thinking that she was in Mexico City.

I realized that she was dead. I imagined her body in parts like a cut sausage, the dead eyes unfocused, the face a bloodless, latex mask. Her mother knew immediately, intuitively. Through networks of family and friends, the question was, "She's dead, isn't she?" Only confirmation was necessary, and the location, and the manner, and the means of responding.

Two weeks later, through a cousin's cousin, we located her body in a morgue in San Luis Potosi, five hours north of Mexico City. They'd found her three days prior in a shipping container in a Walmart parking lot. One of nine dead, with six others half-dead of heat stroke and dehydration, all abandoned by the driver and locked up in the baking 90-degree humidity of the Mexican summer. In the day, the metal box heated up to 120 degrees. "Basically, it was a mobile oven," the police explained. An employee collecting shopping carts heard a faint banging on the door and called the police. They found them there, each without identification, no phones or pictures or luggage. Just bodies. They identified her through her fingerprints taken when she'd crossed over the border four months earlier. They sent pictures, three grainy, immediately deleted pictures, with the desiccated, bruised face barely recognizable in them.

Will was kept at school while we tried to figure out what and how he would be told and how much would be true. I drove for hours thinking about it, trying to craft and shape a message that would cushion and contain the damage. Hours filled with internet searches for appropriate euphemisms for death to tell seven-year-olds. You type in "best ways to tell your child that your spouse is dead," "best places to tell your child that your spouse is dead," "best person to tell your child that your spouse is dead," and Google doesn't give you what you need. A thousand bullshit self-help gurus with living spouses and living, unscarred children and living, unbroken households advise this or that on webpages with names like "Mourning With Your Child" or "Supporting Your Child Through Loss."

His grandmother took it in hand. We picked him up that afternoon, drove him home, sat him down in the living room, and then she told him, in blunt, straightforward language that would've been anathema to any therapist. Not "Mommy's not coming home." Not "Mommy's in heaven." "Mommy died." The essential fact, whether it was comprehensible to a seven-year-old, would have to come into existence for him now.

He received the words passively. She continued. The essential facts, still. She died in Mexico. Eyes down. She was killed trying to get back home to us. Steady breaths. She didn't deserve it. She would've done anything to avoid it. And now, we must remember her with love, but continue, because that's what she would've wanted more than anything.

He said and showed nothing. We sat in silence expecting that, eventually, he would mirror us and cry. For minutes I looked at him, analyzed him, the poker face with baby cheeks.

"Can I go to my room now?" and I returned a nod as he looked up at me, this impenetrable, strong, small thing.

There had to be a funeral, both for decorum and for "healing's" sake. For "closure" to descend on us, a body would have to be seen, be painted up and dressed up and cried and prayed over. It was just as complicated, though, to get a dead body over the border without official permission as a live one. The country was just as on guard, just as inhospitable to the illegal dead as it was to the illegal living. The dead had their bones marked with their native countries, which admitted only those who held the proper passports in their unbending white fingers.

Money. Money makes all things possible. With money, bodies could come back over, under, through the border. With money, they could acquire American citizenship post-mortem.

Through the family, I learned that the cops in San Luis Potosi knew a guy who knew a guy who was just as reputable and respected as the one who had suffocated Marina in the Walmart parking lot. Just the same but with fewer options for murder available to him. For $40,000, he could transfer the body up and out of the country, ensuring that it would be delivered in some manageable state of decay. I wired the cash to an account in Mexico City.

The body traveled from San Luis Potosi by truck to Durango, then into the cargo hold of a passenger plane that conveyed it to Ensenada. And then, from the airport to the port, with "gifts" all around to staff and customs guys and dockworkers. Then, into a fishing boat that headed west into international waters. Once there, it was handed off to another boat with the right provenance that brought it to San Pedro. Then into the flatbed of another truck to our friendly neighborhood funeral parlor.

All the way on ice. On 50 pounds of frequently replaced ice that stuck to the clothes and the skin and the hair. In what looked like a longer and fatter version of a 1980s Igloo cooler. I imagined her sleeping in that box, with beer bottles chilling on her eyelids, on her frosted lashes, banging up against her ribs, chipping away at her teeth. This contraband corpse, battered and bruised.

They let me know when she arrived. The ice had frozen her in a strange, contorted pose, as though she were performing an interpretive dance about a dead body in a cooler rather than being a dead body in a cooler. The funeral director advised against me seeing her. I looked anyway. They laid her on a metal table with a white table cloth, a sheet over her body. Under the sheet, the body's strange terrain was visible, the places where knees and elbows were twisted, where hips had been jarred off course. The head, a dull purple, lay out in the cold, open air.

Chunks of the hair had gone. The remaining strands were matted. The hands had turned to claws. The eyes were pursed shut like two mouths. The lips were black and cracked and swollen. The skin was gray and wrinkled and hard. There were dense bumps on her forehead and bright black bruises imprinted all over her skin. She was a dead animal, unrecognizable, unfamiliar, and the mortuary staff doubted that that they could fully rectify the damage with thawing and lacquer and tricks.

And so, closed casket. A blue, three piece, specially tailored Brioni suit to cover the body. Her dandy, debonair outfit. Silk Hermes pocket square. Silk Hermes tie. Thin, vintage, with little sunflowers on it. A white bespoke dress shirt, the back cut open to fit a body swollen with death. Perfect on her in better times, accentuating all the right parts of a body that had once had all the right parts. A pair of brown Magnanni loafers. Gray socks. All the best, all her favorites and mine. And no one to see any of it. Ever. Not her son. Not her mother, who would've worked herself up into a heart attack if she'd seen what had become of her.

The weeks stretched themselves out in front of us, elongated by errands and sorting out and calls to let people know and constant silences. Marina's mother and the girls moved into a bottom-floor bedroom. They came and went and played in the backyard and prepared meals and watched television shows, with us yet apart from us. Upstairs, across the hallway from one another, we kept our own separate counsels.

He receded from me, the little ghost across the way. Never admitting any emotion, speaking hardly at all, keeping to himself. Now, even with his grandmother and the girls there was no recognition, no attempt to engage. Just the occasional distant look up from the shoes, from the table, from the cereal bowl. He went about the motions as before, numbly up into the car in the morning and then numbly back into the same seat in the afternoon. Down and up the stairs as though no time had elapsed between.

His grandmother and cousins left at the end of the month, back into their own lives and into the business of forgetting. So much easier than trying to inhabit our world, trying to breathe life and vigor and laughter to into it, bridging unbridgeable silences. In their absence, the house became monastic, a cluster of cells with only two occupants. He took his dinner in his room now, on a TV tray that I set up and took down for him. I took him food. I took his plates away when he finished. I drove and pick him up from school.

It wasn't until two or three months later that things began to change. It started at school among peers who had known him before as the lesbians' son and now knew him as the dead lesbians' son. Blood in the water, even in elementary school. He contained it for a time with the same reserve he showed at home.

And then, one day, he snapped. A third grader hassled him during lunch. He didn't say the exact words. He lunged at the boy and grabbed him by his throat, held him for a moment, and then bit his ear and drew blood. Then he headed inside the school as though nothing had happened.

At the school's insistence, I put him in therapy with a woman recommended by the school social worker. Twice a week, Tuesdays, and Thursdays, I drove him 45 minutes on the 210 to Redlands to see her. It didn't seem to make any difference.

Nearly every week, the school called to let me know that he was in trouble again. My assistant would connect the assistant principal or dean or teacher of the hour, the same voices, same beleaguered, annoyed, straining patience. She began to refer to it, mock-comically, as "the usual." And so, every couple of days, "Em, it's the usual," and then ten minutes of my son the bully. He called another boy a faggot. He tore up another kid's work, kicked one of the playground attendants, dumped the contents of his lunch onto the floor in front of a passing custodian. After each, a talking to, after each, a storm of Google searches. "How to talk to your kid about misbehaving." "How to talk to your kid about not being a bully." "How to talk to your kid about grief." "How to talk to your kid."

None of it worked. Whatever glue held other parents and children together, it didn't exist between us and didn't seem to be something that you could manufacture. I tried little outing nights, the movies, sports, playdates. Refusals all around from a boy who wanted to strictly limit his time with me and from parents who wanted to limit their children's time with damaged goods.

I took to yelling at him. "Giving him a talking to," my mother would've said. Chewing him out in the car after picking him up, yet again, from the principal's office. In return, he took to hitting and kicking me, taking out whatever aggression he couldn't give free rein to at school in the privacy of home. Throwing things at me. Sliding his foot in front of my leg as I walked by. Grabbing a fist full of my hair as I drove. I grew accustomed to bruises on my legs. To locking doors behind me.

He made fresh habits of other things, too. Occasionally, I would find him in the morning on the floor, the sheets stained with sweat or urine or both, sometimes bruises or cuts on his head where he'd hit himself in the middle of the night. Occasionally, I would wake in the early morning to the sound of him clanging through the kitchen, tearing pots and pans out of drawers. Other times, just screaming from his room, either high and full of terror or guttural and on the attack. From the window on those nights, I would see neighbors turn on lights, hear them yell out "Christ, not again!" in recognition that it was, yet again, the crazy kid down the street wreaking havoc.

And then, one Wednesday afternoon, he took a wad of paper towels and a butane lighter that he'd taken from a drawer at home, lit the kindling, and dropped it into the trash in an empty classroom. The flames burned high enough to make contact with the old, '70s-style carpeted walls, which breathed them in eagerly. Ten minutes later, a good portion of the school was on fire, with a sizable contingent of emergency vehicles on the scene, a dozen children on their way to the hospital from smoke inhalation, and my son in custody.

They didn't lay out the choice immediately, if you can even call it a choice. They didn't just say, "He can never and will never be allowed to be in a normal school with normal

103

children ever again." In custody, with required supervision even when 1 was visiting with him, they didn't have to.

He turned eight in his first week at the center, in a common room surrounded by boys with similar pasts and identical presents and futures. Boys he'd grow to hate and try to ignore and eventually fight. At the advice of the therapists, a full team now, and at his request, I did not attend. Instead, I had a sheet cake delivered. Vanilla buttercream from his favorite bakery in Covina, with a picture of him and Marina printed on its surface.

GREAT SILENCE

West Park, New York

I felt that this place was made for me—both remote and proximate, far enough to forget, close enough to admit the gentlest reminders of others. I felt that it would allow me to disappear. Both to the world and to myself. I felt that I might find forgiveness here. I loved it for that reason.

I particularly loved the Great Silence, the period of quiet between 8:30 in the evening and 8:30 the next morning. In the stillness, I could hear the cicadas in the trees, the distant sounds of cars and ships, the gentle rolling of the river. I could listen to the voices of the past, talk to God, to myself, to my conscience. All without being required to interact, without feeling compelled to give anything to anyone else. A selfish, self-contained life. A dream life, always drifting above, beneath, someplace else.

In summer or winter, I would sit as the rain and snow came down, observe the landscape reinvent itself as Russia or Vietnam, watch the Hudson become the Volga or the Mekong. Watch and imagine. Watch and forget. I came here for that.

There were many paths to this place. I seemed to be the only one who came from nothing.

The rest came from New York, Boston, Philadelphia, San Francisco. From university life, media, tech, marriage and family. Several of the brothers fit one or more of these categories. There was a former Latin American literature professor from Bowdoin. There was a former editor at *Harper's*. There were brothers who studied law, who taught music in elite high schools in the Northeast. Brothers who dallied with progressive activism, who chained themselves to gates or to the back ends of buses bound for resettlement processing centers. There was a young man who helped co-found three or four apps in Silicon Valley.

They broke and came here, just like me. They, all of them, were true believers, men for whom the words of the Matins service, the endless psalms, the canticles, the daily Magnificat were new and fresh each morning. They aspired to holiness in the same way that they once aspired to promotions at work. All in.

We didn't speak about the past very often. The circle of offices and meals and chores made conversation blessedly infrequent, and none of us came here to build deep relationships with other people. Quite the contrary.

When we did congregate and talk, the other, more eager brothers took the floor and shared stories of their lives until we all sank into an unspoken funk of nostalgia and regret and self-doubt. And then some more quiet, more distracted person—one of the old guard who had come here before recent events had made monastic life fashionable—turned the conversation, pushed us back into devout silence. Often I fulfilled this role, the turner, the obscurer, the speaker of the blessed words, "Enough talk."

And so, after four years in residence here, I came to know most of the brothers' stories, while none of them came to know mine. If pushed, easy fictions appeared on my lips. Even the prior had been provided a heavily revised version of my life. He found it convincing enough to stop asking questions.

That July, my fourth here, was typical enough. The house was half-empty, just the brothers and the few heartier guests from the city who could endure the triple-digit humidity with nothing but cheap old fans as consolation. They huddled up in the common rooms and the library (the only public room with a working wall unit), reading, sweating, napping, playing board games.

Monastic time in July and August always lengthened. There was an absence of religious catharsis, nothing to really prepare for or anticipate. It was too hot to work outside. It was too stifling indoors to really focus on any activity. Eyes wandered from the pages of books. Cleaning and mending and copying and praying were all done poorly. Contemplation was made more difficult by the dripping and dissolving of one's own flesh. The smell of body odor filled everything.

Days filled with rain and thunder. Water came down in sheets and we watched it from behind windows, with the roof dripping on our foreheads and the carpets growing damp and earth-scented. When the rain stopped, we sopped the floors and fanned them to head off the growth of mildew and mold.

In bed at night, the biting of bugs and scratching of limbs. Ticks and fleas and mosquitos in the air and in the mattresses. Bedbugs, of course, always. Nothing to do about that. All that one can do is accept the red parts reddening, accept that flesh turns pink and blistered and swollen, that it is prey to things in the earth and the air that feed on it throughout life and then consume it totally in death.

In the chapel, packed in five times a day, the crucified Christ bled with sweat. In particularly severe rainstorms, the hundred-year-old roof creaked and dripped, drizzling bibles and prayer books with so much water that the prior decided to make copies of the readings and stash the books away for safe-keeping. Compline and the darkness after couldn't come soon enough. Most of the brothers would shuffle off to bed soon after, disappearing into prayer or reading or sleep.

I used this time to escape to the crypt, the burial place of brothers back to the 1880s. The bodies now numbered around 110, most dead before the two wars, when the order had burgeoned with young immigrant men from New York City, attracted to the romantic simplicity of the monastic life and the easy security of three square meals and free lodging.

No one came here now except for the housekeepers. It was, in a world of quiet and seclusion, the most quiet and secluded place on offer.

The main crypt chapel was large and dark and round and carpeted. It felt like a womb. It smelled of mushrooms. It was used only three times a year, on the Feast Day of St. Benedict, the Feast Day of the Exaltation of the Holy Cross, and on All Souls' Day, when we recited the names of all the dead brothers and imagined our names among them. The rest of the year, it sat empty. Off this room was a ring of separate, enclosed shrines to the Virgin, the Sacred Heart, St. Jude, and the Holy Cross.

After Compline, I made my rounds, prayed a bit to each statue and then sat and thought in the quiet. My prayers were earnest and thorough. Prayers for enlightenment, for distant, semi-forgotten family, for the dead. Prayers for forgiveness. Always, always for that. I imagined God nodding impatiently through it all, already knowing the words, bored to death of them.

Late one night that July, as I finished up my round of prayers, I looked up to find a man standing at the bottom of the stairs that led down from the main chapel. He looked like any other summer "pilgrim" in shorts and a t-shirt, here to hike and sight-see and explore some vague idea of "spirituality." He stood motionless, examining me like a curiosity.

"Can I help you, young man?" I asked him. The pastoral voice of authority.

He shook his head and then walked back up the stairs.

The next morning, my eyes aching in the harsh dawn light, I took my appointed place in the choir. In the quiet before the Matins bell rang, I saw the man enter. In the light, I realized he was much older than I'd initially thought. Around 40, with a streak of gray in his hair.

We sang. "Glory to the Father and to the Son and to the Holy Spirit," and then went straight into Psalm 22, led by Brother Jordan's high, pure voice. One of the "woe is me, take vengeance on them" psalms, the psalmist sitting in the ruins, his family dead, his country enslaved. Familiar words, in the strange, ethereal countertenor of the one among us who knew the least about pain, who had the least cause to mourn. He'd gone straight from college to seminary to the house. He sang the words of the Psalm with far too much kindness, with a smile on his soft, unlined, 20-something face.

My eyes drifted from him to the crypt man. He had a sun-damaged, unpleasant wear about him, the cragginess of the escaped convict, his skin dried out like leather. I imagined the voice that went with the face. Here was a man who could say the words "I am poured out like water, and all my bones are disjointed; my heart is like wax, melting within me" and be believed. His eyes looked back at me from their boney coffers. They focused and held me, sharp and precise and hostile. I turned from him to my prayer book and then looked up again. He was gone.

The day was humid but not unbearably so. I disappeared into it. I walked about a mile down the trail that led along the Hudson, down a set of old, termite-worn wood stairs, through a gray, ghostly section of woods. Bark beetles had taken out large sections of the forest here. They'd nested in the trunks, coring them, burrowing into the trees' hearts. The trees were now stone pillars, buckling and crumbling ruins. I found them very beautiful.

I'd often come here in the afternoons, down a broken path segmented by fallen sections of trees, strewn with piles of gray, decaying needles. Come here and sit and dream on the bench.

I had always had places like this, quiet, secret places, sectioned off from others, as far away from the human voice as possible. One of the only things that I'd enjoyed about Redlands was the abundance of such places. Through the gate after work or even on my lunch breaks, it was ten minutes into the San Bernardino Mountains. It was possible to drive there and park and wander and get lost, but never in the same place. It was a perfect solitude, a forgetting chamber.

Necessary there. More than any other place I'd ever been, necessary there.

And necessary here, too. In the stone circle, feet on the bench, I dozed, lulled by the sounds of the river and the woods.

Hours later, I awoke. My tongue was dry and sour. My skin stung. The sun was overhead. I had slept through most of the day, through three of the five offices. I heard bells in the distance, announcing the approach of vespers. The other brothers would already be filing in, already opening their breviaries and silently mouthing their private, preparatory prayers.

I scrambled up the stairs and down the path. In the heat, drowning in sweat, I went as fast as my legs could take me. What usually took me twenty-five minutes to cover took me ten, and I cleared the woods and crossed over onto the lawn. I dreaded what awaited me, the disapproval that lay in store. Extra duties would be assigned as a means of instructing me in this lesson, something tailored to my dislikes, like taking over the role of guestmaster or writing sermons for the next month. In rule and in practice, brothers did not miss services and were not late for them. Any instance when they did was treated as a dereliction of duty. And I'd missed three.

As I crossed the lawn in the direction of the chapel, a figure ran down in the opposite direction to meet me. It moved quickly, directly toward me. It was the man from the crypt, holding a long black object in his left hand. I stopped and looked around me. There was no one. All the brothers were at prayer. All the guests were readying themselves for the service or were in their rooms or out wandering the Vanderbilt or Roosevelt grounds.

He came face to face with me there, with the gun in his hand. "I know you," he said.

"And I know you," I replied.

Years before, I had called him the Marlboro Man. He wore a cartoon Stetson and a bolo tie. He had a sun-damaged, tobacco-worn, booze-damaged face and a Sam Elliot voice. He was a semi-regular visitor to the center; not the type to come every week, with guilt and shame on their faces, but a few-times-a-year parent, in for a day just to check the box on the list and move on.

By the time I began working in his ward, the son was universally considered a hopeless case. He was 13 years old but small for his age. He still had a child's manner and a child's face. He was biracial, with a hint of red in his uncut curls. He'd been in for about two or three years by that point, taken out of school for some infraction or another.

Since then, he'd quickly descended the rungs of restriction, from "normal" to "support" to "intensive support" and now, into the "individualized" unit. Here, each resident was kept to himself in a small, locked room that admitted the outside world through a coke bottle-thick glass window the size of a piece of paper.

He had a reputation for violence by that point, inflicted on himself and others, on other residents and staff. Opportunistic violence, the chance sensed and seized in the second's time that another person exposed her or himself to him. Biting or scratching or slamming the door shut on fingers or hands. Slamming himself into cinder block walls or collapsing on floors until restrained and sedated by staff. By that point, we'd dispensed with the behavioral specialists and the 1-on-1s, had cut most of the instructional and special programs, at least for the kids who weren't showing obvious signs of improvement. What remained for them, for him, was maybe an hour of "tutoring" through the window, with a laminated sheet and a soft, felt-tipped pen handed to him to do math problems or write responses to questions fed to him through the speaker by one of the on-call "teachers" making the rounds. Life—meals, clothing, knowledge, news—came and went through the speakers and a small slot in the door.

And each day, an hour outside in the grassy atrium that lay at the heart of the ward with the other 11 boys, all damaged, all locked up in their own rooms until the "recess hour" came.

After the first six months or so, those who hadn't come broken learned how to be. They learned it was expected, that it was natural in such a place. Progressively, they gave up pieces of themselves—trying to keep occupied, taking exercise, passing notes or yelling into the adjoining rooms—until they resembled animals, snarling and scratching at the world. Whether they chose or didn't choose, whatever they became in however long it took them to become it, the treatment would be the same: deprived of all but the smallest, sparsest pieces of life, cut off from the world.

They were allowed visitors once a week for two hours in a visitation room off the central ward that was comfortable and normal looking, with a lumpy brown sectional couch that suggested the most lived-in of living rooms. A shelf on the wall was filled with books and game boxes and ancient DVDs and videogame disks. A scratched up, decade-old flat screen television connected to various videogame consoles. Parents would be escorted into the room prior to the residents, after contents of pockets and purses were inspected and emptied and the necessary waivers were signed excusing the company of liability in case their child harmed them on the premises. That was a regular occurrence, even in the presence of the guards. It was not unusual for a child to enter, all sweetness and light, glad to see his mother, and then take a contraband shiv out of his pocket and stab her.

Each of the parents had signed paperwork that specified the limits of their rights. Rights to visit. Rights to communicate with their child with 24 hours' notice. Rights to speak with concerned educational staff and to be informed of academic results and progress. Rights to remove their child at any time on the condition that they would lose their place in the facility and would be placed at the end of the waiting list should they want to readmit him. In my time there, only two parents removed their children: one for placement in an even more restrictive facility and the other for a new age religious program in New Mexico. Both later tried to return.

For the most part, the parents of the children in our "care" were pleased with the services that they received, happy to deposit their children and forget them.

When I met the Marlboro man, I had been on staff two years. I'd applied many years before, one of thousands who had submitted multiple resumes and cover letters and recommendations in the thin hope that I'd be called back for the grand prize of a stable job and health insurance and retirement benefits. John and I had been married for four years by that point, scraping by in his mother's house in Rancho on his teacher's salary and welfare checks, most of which went towards servicing student loans that we could hope to realistically pay off sometime in the 2050s. He had urged me toward it, said that they were looking for folks with experience in social work.

And so, after years bouncing from temporary gig to temporary gig, buying nothing, spending nothing, our otherwise happy marriage straining under the weight of his effort and my inability, when the call came and the offer was extended— Support Provider, $45,000 a year with full benefits, at the Poitrain Holistic Care Center in Redlands— I took it without asking questions. You took what you could get, whatever you could get. And when the job was long-term and 40 hours a week and putatively middle class, you bowed your head and thanked God for it.

They put me in the support unit first with kids who were struggling but still normal. My task was to keep them occupied, to locate interests and activate them, to organize events that would make the unit seem like a proper community. Most of the kids had been through an incident or two while in the regular residential program, verbally lashed out against others or against staff, maybe refused to obey curfew or stolen food. Most were just plain depressed, bored, uninspired to do much beyond sit around in the common areas or in their rooms on their phones all day, playing games or texting friends who'd been placed in other facilities. But, even so, they still did normal kid things. They still attended classes in a proper room designated for lessons, working through online units in regular subjects. They still formed friendships and crushes, ate meals, went to the garden or the field to laze in the sun or read. I could pretend that I worked at a boarding school, a boring, unprestigious, institutional boarding school where most of the kids were manageable and even pleasant when properly engaged.

My six months there were bearable. It was uninspiring work. I spent most of the time either doing paperwork, documenting my observations of Resident 1438's day or Resident 1398's verbal altercation with Resident 1421, or trying to talk with kids who had little interest in relating to someone whom they knew was paid to take an interest. I didn't form meaningful relationships, either positive or negative. But it was harmless work, purposeless and victimless, and the result at the end of every two weeks was more than enough to keep me in it. Other members of the staff had similar attitudes—no attachments, good or bad, either to the residents or to each other. It was just a paycheck. It seemed to suit us all just fine.

My supervisor was a girl in her early 20s, just as benign and nonchalant as the rest of us, straight from business school. In a constellation of lackluster employees, I had become a default favorite, distinguished from the rest by a graduate degree and the fact that I did care, to a certain degree, about the kids, did try to smile and talk to them. Towards the end of the year, she made the decision—without consulting me—to put me in for an opening in the individualized ward, where my salary would be supplemented by a $10,000 bonus that was roundly referred to as "hazard pay." I was happy enough to accept and ignorant of what it entailed.

Another world lay on the other edge of the campus in a four-story building behind a chain link fence. It was smallest of the units. The staff was all-male. Most had backgrounds in security, either as cops or as guards or as former military. Most looked at the kids with snarling disdain, both bored and disgusted by them.

From the beginning, I was the odd man out, the softie fluke whose transfer had obviously been a mistake. I would learn. I would be forced to learn. They—the residents—would teach me.

The first year was an agony of loneliness and guilt and stifled outrage. The unit was a daily funeral, a place where boys were buried, thrown into cells to be forgotten. Most said nothing through the day, nothing but grunts and snarls. They were objects to be thrown around, to be strong-armed in and out of doorways. When they did bite or kick or punch back, the payback would come quickly, a thick arm around a throat and then hard against the concrete floor with a thud. Regardless of whether the boy was 8 or 18, regardless of whether he was 4'7" or 6'7".

By far, he was the worst, both in his behavior and in his treatment. Daily, the food tray would go in and get thrown and then, in response, a guard would come in through the door and pound away at him. Later, through the little observation window on the door, I'd watch him sit on the plastic mattress, his knees gathered up in his arms, staring at the wall in anticipation of the inevitable entrance of the guards to force feed him.

I watched and didn't watch, watched and grew adept at obscuring. Most days, I'd take long lunch breaks, leave the grounds in my car, go up into the mountains or just idle on some decaying suburban street with a cigarette and have a stab at blankness, try to empty out the contents of the morning and to preemptively forget whatever was to come in the afternoon. I never mentioned anything about work at home. Instead, the mask would come off at the end of the day and another would replace it in the evenings so that I could comfortably talk about houses or vacations or anniversary plans.

The father came maybe three times the entire time I was there. Each visit was an event, a topic of discussion. "Hey, you'll never guess whose father is here to see him." Each lasted minutes until the boy did something violent to end it and a guard dragged him back into the cell where he belonged, where he would always belong.

I was only present in the room at the last visit.

We didn't bother with the "We care about your child" act with him. He knew the kind of treatment his child got here. I brought the boy in restraints, his small hands zip-tied behind his back. I took him down in the elevator and into the room, with his father nervously waiting for him, seated at a table with his hands folded. I nodded to him as we entered but said nothing as I took my seat in a chair in the corner, ten feet or so from them.

The man received his son with a hug, pulling the stiff body into his arms. The leathery hand came up to the boy's chin, and the father offered a compliment on his son's handsomeness as he completed a cursory examination. His mother was mentioned, spoken of in passing. She sent her regards. The father turned in my direction, nodding, the signal to release, to cut the plastic around the wrists.

I took the pair of safety scissors on my belt—a special plastic guard on the blades to impede the boys from using them in any of the ways that they might dream up—and cut at the white plastic, revealing the chafed wrists where the boy had tried to pull and grind himself out of them. Slowly, unsteadily, the hands came around to his front, as father and son went to their places on the opposite sides of the table and I returned to my corner.

The father tried banter, questions and answers. The hows and whats and whens of a life that he obviously knew very little about and obviously didn't really care to understand.

"How's it going? How are all your friends doing?" As if there were new developments. As if friendships could be conducted through cinderblock walls and shatterproof, soundproof glass. The boy's groggy silence was sufficient answer.

We tried to find a balance in sedating the boys for visits, a precise measure of downness, just enough to effect docility while leaving them the capacity to think and talk. The boy seemed to have been drugged way too much to produce speech, let alone to act like a normal child meeting with a father that he hadn't seen in months. He slumped in his chair. That he kept sitting without collapsing on the floor was an accomplishment. The father didn't seem to notice, continued with questions and updates without even a grunt or a returned look in response.

Ten minutes passed. The father continued with the monologue, kept with life as it was lived without son, with mother and siblings and house and school and work and grandparents and old friends. I imagined it as a long-form letter written to a dead relative, like a poem thrown in the trash, like a novel never published, a purgative, an exercise, performed for the performer's benefit. He didn't stop until the son's elbows gave way and the face fell on the wooden tabletop with a dull thump.

"Help me wake him up, will ya?" he said to me. "Come on. Help me with him. Help me get him sat up for me."

Forty-five minutes and a fresh zip tie later, I hauled the boy back to his cell, his limp body in my arms, his eyes closed. The mannequin had been said goodbye to without its knowledge. It had been propped up for the purpose. Three or four times. My hands pushed it up into place, moving the plastic torso until it complied. In return, the father gave me a quick thank you and left through doors that eagerly opened to him, out into a world his son could not, would not ever know.

I pulled the boy into his cell and onto the thin blue plastic mat that served as the only furniture in the room. He grunted as I lifted his legs up on to it, his whole body little more than half the length of the full bed.

And then I left work. Without asking. Without clocking out, with three hours to go on my shift. I went up into the mountains, leaving the car on the side of the road around a turn that left it wide open for an easy collision. Didn't care. The sun was going down, but the air was still hot and humid. I wandered into a patch of trees—dried, grey things, products of the same bark beetles that would follow me back east years later. I sat down in the dark like a child, knees in my arms, head against the cheap, shiny-smooth cotton of my uniform pants, feeling further than ever before from myself, from whatever ideals and constants I thought I had established for myself. I felt a thousand miles away from John and parents and friends and upbringings and values and days when I had been outraged at acts of brutality that other people did that I now did myself and excused.

The next week was an infinity, an uneasy, indefinite slog of private thoughts and private misgivings and vague notions that something, something must be done to set this right. I felt pulled to his room throughout the day, pulled to look through the open window, to check on him. It seemed to fill the building, to define it: this boy's pain, mistreatment, abuse. This was the place where it happened. It was in the ceiling beams and the fluorescent lights and the drywall and the bones of the staff; we all conspired to make it happen. We all contributed to it. It was our central story. It was who we were.

Later in the week, I was assigned meal duty. I loaded up the cart with the boxed meals and the bags of safety utensils and cups, filled the trays, poured the boys their cups of water, placed the boxes and sporks and napkins and cups neatly on top. I unlocked the slots in the doors, slid the trays in, watched just long enough to see whether the boys started eating, let the evening crew know so that they could pass over or prepare to force feed them.

I made my rounds, saving him for last. I picked up the microwaved TV dinner and slid it through. He sat on the ground, as he always did, staring off through windows that weren't there in walls that were.

The hallway was empty. I unlocked the door and went into the boy's cell. He didn't look up, kept his eyes where they were fixed. I looked at him: the matted hair, the soiled clothes, the bruises on his arms and face. I looked at the room: the hard, gray surfaces, the suffocating closeness and darkness, the plastic mat and the metal toilet in the corner and the untouched tray of food on the ground. And then I looked back at a plastic bag of cups on the cart, pulled the remaining cups out, placed the empty bag down on the ground, turned, left, and locked the room.

He didn't use it immediately. When they came in to force feed him that night, they found him there, the bag nowhere in evidence.

It was sometime in the night when he put it over his head and tied it off around his neck. It must've taken discipline and endurance to get it right, to resist the urge to pull it open and breathe, mindful that there was no second chance, no other bag to use. He must've struggled to keep his arms from tearing at it. Somehow, he forced them down, resisted every instinct. He did it in silence, in the gap between bed checks, with steadiness and resolve.

I left Redlands maybe a month after that, just long enough after to avoid any undue suspicion. They hadn't reported the plastic bag; instead, they said he'd suffocated himself with the bed mat. Found a way to secretly, slyly cut it up and take the cloth and tie it around his neck like a noose.

I gave my notice. Personal reasons. The severance was almost nothing, just enough to make it through the next few months. But it was sufficient for my purposes. John and I sped through the divorce in record time, easily, undramatically, with nothing to divide, with my claims given up and the only

119

remaining possession a small account with the few dollars that I'd made by and for myself. He was, after years of poorly concealed disinterest and depression, largely happy to see the back of me, and even happier that I was content to surrender up the house.

I'd already discovered Holy Cross, already made my intentions known to the prior through email and by telephone, already made the initial arrangements to relocate to West Park and start the process that had led here, to this vocation, to this house and this lawn and this afternoon and to the comfortable but false notion that I could make a clean break from what had come before, that I could escape causes and effects, acts and consequences.

And now, here he was, the boy's long-lost father. The end of the line of causation, sweating and twitching in front of me, with his gun in my face. He repeated himself. "I know you."

I nodded. "Yes. Yes, you do."

In the distance, I could hear them, the brothers, those white robed mimics of the saints. I could hear Brother Jordan's high voice coming down the hill, leading them in the litany. It was Psalm 51. "Purge me with hyssop, and I shall be clean: wash me, and I shall be whiter than snow." His words floated in the air, too pure sounding to seem human, too angelic to sound like they might apply to me.

Christopher Records is a writer and poet from Riverside, California. He has written four unpublished novels and numerous pieces of poetry and prose that have been published in *The Rumpus, Entropy Magazine, Homology Lit*, and other publications. *Care: Stories* is his first published book. Follow him on Twitter or Instagram at @cdrecords001.

ABOUT INLANDIA INSTITUTE

Inlandia Institute is a regional non-profit and literary center. We seek to bring focus to the richness of the literary enterprise that has existed in this region for ages. The mission of the Inlandia Institute is to recognize, support, and expand literary activity in all of its forms in Inland Southern California by publishing books and sponsoring programs that deepen people's awareness, understanding, and appreciation of this unique, complex and creatively vibrant region.

The Institute publishes books, presents free public literary and cultural programming, provides in-school and after school enrichment programs for children and youth, holds free creative writing workshops for teens and adults, and boot camp intensives. In addition, every two years, the Inlandia Institute appoints a distinguished jury panel from outside of the region to name an Inlandia Literary Laureate who serves as an ambassador for the Inlandia Institute, promoting literature, creative literacy, and community. Laureates to date include Susan Straight (2010-2012), Gayle Brandeis (2012-2014), Juan Delgado (2014-2016), Nikia Chaney (2016-2018), and Rachelle Cruz (2018-2020).

To learn more about the Inlandia Institute, please visit our website at www.InlandiaInstitute.org.

INLANDIA BOOKS

San Bernardino, Singing, by Nikia Chaney

Facing Fire: Art, Wildfire, and the End of Nature in the New West by Douglas McCulloh

Writing from Inlandia: Work from the Inlandia Creative Writing Workshops, an annual anthology

In the Sunshine of Neglect: Defining Photographs and Radical Experiments in Inland Southern California, 1950 to the Present by Douglas McCulloh

Henry L. A. Jekel: Architect of Eastern Skyscrapers and the California Style by Dr. Vincent Moses and Catherine Whitmore

Orangelandia: The Literature of Inland Citrus by Gayle Brandeis

While We're Here We Should Sing by The Why Nots

Go to the Living by Micah Chatterton

No Easy Way: Integrating Riverside Schools - A Victory for Community by Arthur L. Littleworth

HILLARY GRAVENDYK PRIZE BOOKS

The Silk the Moths Ignore by Bronwen Tate
Winner of the 2019 National Hillary Gravendyk Prize

Remyth: A Postmodernist Ritual by Adam Martinez
Winner of the 2019 Regional Hillary Gravendyk Prize

Former Possessions of the Spanish Empire by Michelle Peñaloza
Winner of the 2018 National Hillary Gravendyk Prize

All the Emergency-Type Structures by Elizabeth Cantwell
Winner of the 2018 Regional Hillary Gravendyk Prize

Our Bruises Kept Singing Purple by Malcolm Friend
Winner of the 2017 National Hillary Gravendyk Prize

Traces of a Fifth Column by Marco Maisto
Winner of the 2016 National Hillary Gravendyk Prize

God's Will for Monsters by Rachelle Cruz
Winner of the 2016 Regional Hillary Gravendyk Prize
Winner of a 2018 American Book Award

Map of an Onion by Kenji C. Liu
Winner of the 2015 National Hillary Gravendyk Prize

All Things Lose Thousands of Times by Angela Peñaredondo
Winner of the 2015 Regional Hillary Gravendyk Prize